SAVAGE SHOWDOWN

Mooney kicked Clint's gun aside and threw himself on the Gunsmith. They rolled, punching, gouging and clawing. Mooney savagely drove his thumbs up into Clint's face, searching for his eye sockets.

On the edge of losing consciousness, the Gunsmith kicked up his heels, wrapped them around Mooney's neck and jerked the man over backward. Dimly, he could hear the roar of the flames and feel the heat of the fire.

Mooney jumped up toward his coat hanging on his bedpost and yanked a two-shot derringer from one of his pockets. Before he could raise the derringer, Clint grabbed his wrist and they struggled for control of the weapon until the derringer exploded between their bodies with a muffled roar . . .

*   *   *

SPECIAL PREVIEW!

Turn to the back of this book for a sneak-peek excerpt
of the new epic western series . . .

THE HORSEMEN

. . . the sprawling, unforgettable story of a
family of horse breeders and trainers—from the
Civil War South to the Wild West.

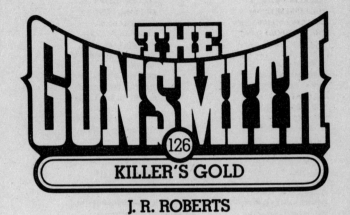

THE GUNSMITH

126

KILLER'S GOLD

J. R. ROBERTS

JOVE BOOKS, NEW YORK

KILLER'S GOLD

A Jove Book / published by arrangement with
the author

PRINTING HISTORY
Jove edition / June 1992

ISBN: 0-515-10867-7

THE GUNSMITH

126

KILLER'S GOLD

ONE

To the Gunsmith's way of thinking, it seemed like a man's luck could fall into a slide and there was nothing he could do except ride it all the way to the bottom. At least, that's the way Clint Adams's luck had gone after losing most of his money playing faro in Prescott, Arizona. Things went from bad to worse two days later when his fine black gelding, Duke, threw a shoe and went lame.

Now, broke and with Duke still limping painfully, a weary Gunsmith was leading his horse across the Arizona high country toward a mining and ranching town named Quartz. From all accounts, Quartz was just a couple of dilapidated saloons, a general store, livery, and a few mining and ranching supply outfits. The only thing that Quartz did have worth mentioning was the finest whorehouse in northern Arizona.

Even that did not hold any excitement for the Gunsmith after this long, tiring day. Besides, he was almost broke, and as he at last topped a low rise to survey Quartz he shook his head and said, "Duke, it's going to be tough to get back on our feet in a place as poor-looking as this."

Duke flicked his ears back and forth. The big horse was in pain, and Clint cussed the traveling drummer who'd taken his last few dollars for a couple of bottles of worthless liniment.

1

It took almost another hour for the Gunsmith to arrive on the outskirts of town. In tune with the bad luck that had been plaguing his every step, the first thing to greet him was a massive dog that came flying out from beside a miner's shack. The beast had its hackles raised and its teeth bared. Clint resisted the urge to just shoot the damn thing. Instead, he scooped a rock from the street, took aim, and hurled the missile. The rock hit the attacking dog between the eyes, and the snarling animal did a flip, then climbed groggily to its feet.

"Get out of here!" Clint shouted, scooping up a second rock.

The dog recovered its senses sufficiently to streak off down the dusty street with its tail between its legs.

"Nice shot," a woman called.

Clint turned back toward town to see Quartz's famous whorehouse. It was a sunny afternoon in midweek, and things must have been slow, because the girls were sitting on the porch sunning themselves and watching him with more than a little interest.

"Well thank you," Clint said, cheered a little by the girl's smile as he continued on up the street.

The girl said, "Honey, you look hard used. Why don't you stop awhile and let little Annabelle revive your weary body."

Clint chuckled. "I'm afraid I'm a little poor in the pocket today, Annie. Maybe another time."

"Wouldn't cost a handsome man like you much on such a slow day," the girl said. "A dollar would be fine."

"Even a dollar is more than I can spare right now," Clint admitted. "But if my luck changes, who knows?"

"Yeah," she said, glancing over her shoulder toward her companions. "You just be sure and ask for me, honey. Not one of these vultures standing in the wings. Hear now?"

"Sure," Clint said as the other women gave them both a good razing.

The girls watched him, some of them making catcalls and offering their services free, though probably only in sport. Clint paid them no mind. He continued on into town and was almost run down when a carriage came swinging around a corner, moving too fast.

The driver was a black man dressed like a Mississippi riverboat gambler, with a black suit, white shirt, and tie. He sawed hard on the reins and swerved on by Clint, who turned to yell at him in anger.

"Mr. Washington, stop!" a woman's voice called from inside the coach.

The driver brought the carriage to a halt, and the door flew open to reveal a very pretty woman with blond hair and a splash of red lipstick.

"Are you all right?" she asked, poking her head out the door.

"I am," Clint said, "but no thanks to your driver."

"Mr. Washington," she said, looking up at the black man, "I've told you time and again not to be in such a hurry!"

The black man did not look overly concerned. "Yes, Miss Lucy," he said.

The woman turned back to Clint, started to say something, then frowned.

"What's the matter?" he asked.

"Nothing. But I've seen you someplace before."

"I've been a lot of places, Miss Lucy. But if I'd seen you, I'd have remembered. You're not the kind a man with good eyes would ever forget."

The woman took Clint's words for the compliment he'd intended. "So, do you like what you're seeing?"

"Who wouldn't?"

The woman shrugged in reply. "I *have* seen you someplace before. But it was in a big city and you were . . . were well dressed, shaved and . . ."

She smiled. "Yes, and you were playing poker and winning big." Her eyebrows arched. "It doesn't appear that you've won big for quite some time now."

Clint felt his cheeks warm with anger. "Everyone has to take the bad times along with the good. And I'm glad to see that one as pretty as you is having good times."

Clint tipped his hat and started to move on into town.

"Wait, please!"

He stopped, turned, and saw her emerge from the carriage. She was tall and slender in the waist and hips, but full breasted.

"I didn't mean to be arrogant sounding or cruel," she said. "And you're right. Things are going very well for me. I own the house just up the street that you must have noticed."

"The one with the girls?"

"Yes."

That surprised him. Miss Lucy was definitely a cut above most frontier madams. She looked like the wife of a banker or the town doctor. But then, one thing he'd learned was never to judge people by their appearances.

"You're the Gunsmith! Now I remember!"

"That's right."

"Pardon me for saying so, but you look in need of money and I just happen to need a personal bodyguard. One that can use a gun better than my enemies."

"Sorry," Clint said. "I'm not a bounty hunter, a pimp, or a bodyguard."

"What are you except broke?"

"I'm hungry, out of sorts, and leading a lame horse."

"I can help."

"Not interested in being a bodyguard," he said. "I'll find other work hereabouts."

"It would be a mistake to count on that."

"Well," Clint said, "mistakes are part of living. I like to make my own choices."

Before Miss Lucy could argue the point, Clint tipped his dusty black hat and continued on into Quartz. As he passed up the street, he saw that at least a dozen of the citizens had witnessed his entrance and probably, if they'd strained, even heard his exchange with Miss Lucy. That would account for their silly-looking grins.

To hell with them, Clint thought, heading down the street toward the town's only livery. But just before he reached it, Miss Mullane's carriage got there first.

"I hope you'll reconsider my offer," she said. "My life really is in danger, and I would pay you well. Also those in my employment receive some excellent benefits. Isn't that right, Mr. Washington?"

The driver flashed a wide grin to reveal a perfect set of teeth. "Yessum, Miss Mullane!"

"I'll bet," Clint said.

They left a few minutes later and Clint found the liveryman unharnessing the carriage. "Afternoon," he said, extending his hand.

"Afternoon," the stableman said, giving his hand a quick pump. "What can I do for you?"

"I need a stall, some doctorin' for my horse and lots of hay and grain."

The man rubbed his whiskered face. He walked over to Duke and crouched by his lame foot, then raised and inspected the hoof carefully. "Bruised frog," he grunted. "Going to take time and liniment."

"I've already used liniment."

"What kind?"

"Doc Wright's Horse Liniment."

"Hell," the liveryman snorted, "Doc Wright is nothing but a two-bit snake oil peddler. I've got some *real* horse liniment. Bought it from the Indians and you'll never find any better. They've got their native medicines that have been around for centuries. They know secrets we'll never understand."

"How much?"

"It's expensive. I'll also have to soak that hoof so the liniment will enter the frog. Probably ought to use some on the tendons as well. Lame horse stretches them out wrong.

Could ruin a fine horse like this forever if he ain't doctored right."

"How much?" Clint repeated.

"Fifty dollars."

"Fifty dollars!"

The liveryman shrugged. He was a short but very powerfully built man in his forties. "Nothin' in life is cheap. And if you can't afford to take care of a fine animal, maybe you could talk me into paying . . . oh, twenty dollars for him."

"I wouldn't sell him to you for five hundred," Clint snapped.

"Lame horse without care and treatment isn't worth anything," the liveryman sighed. "Now, since we've no business to do together, I've got things to do."

"Wait!" Clint lowered his voice. "Listen, maybe we got off on the wrong foot with each other. I'm pretty handy. How about I work off my horse's board bill? I could . . ."

"Sorry, but I'm not interested," the liveryman said. "I don't need any extra help. Besides, when we first shook hands, I noticed you've never been a working man. Not with those soft hands."

"I can use a rake, shovel, pick or ax when I have to," Clint said indignantly.

"Well, with me, you won't have to because I don't need help. You bring in fifty dollars, we can work something out for that horse."

Clint turned away in anger and led Duke back outside. He wanted to tell this liveryman exactly what he could do with his fifty dollars.

Clint looked up and down Quartz's main street. "I'll find work someplace," he promised the horse. "And I'll get fifty dollars so we can get that hoof healed. After that, we'll put this sorry damn town behind us and never look back."

Duke nickered in soft agreement and Clint led the animal on up the street and tied it before the Ace High Saloon.

He'd done bartending a time or two, and it was easier work than cleaning stalls. Besides, if he could get a few dollars together, there was bound to be a small stakes poker game that he could join.

"With a little luck, we'll be back on our feet in no time at all," he told Duke before he stepped into the saloon.

TWO

It wasn't much of a saloon to speak of and there wasn't much business either. Just ten or twelve bored-looking cowboys and miners either standing at the bar or playing some low-stakes poker.

When Clint walked into the Ace High, almost no one bothered to pay attention to him because he looked like a hundred other down-and-out men passing through Quartz.

Clint cocked his heel on the brass rail and leaned on the bartop. "I'd like a beer," he said to a tall, skinny bartender with a mustache that was ridiculously long and waxed at the tips.

The bartender had been talking to a couple of miners, and when Clint interrupted a joke he was telling, the bartender shot him a go-to-hell look, then resumed telling his joke.

Clint was long on broke and short on patience. He gave the bartender a thirty-second grace period. Then he peeled away from the bar, took three long steps down its length, and reached out to grab the bartender by the shirtfront.

"Hey!" one of the miners protested. "What the . . ."

Something in Clint's eyes made him swallow whatever next he was going to say.

Clint jerked the cadaverous bartender right up on his toes.

"Let go of me, damn you! Are you crazy or something!"

9

"No, I'm tired and I'm thirsty and by damned if I'm going to wait until some third-rate, piss-ant bartender like you is ready to pour me a beer!"

At that, Clint slapped the man with his open palm. Hit him once going left and then came back and belted him going right.

The bartender's head rocked twice and a trickle of blood ran down his chin. He was wearing an apron. Under it was a two-shot derringer he tried to yank free.

That made the Gunsmith even angrier and he belted the man in his solar plexis, right under his rib cage, where it hurt something awful to take a hard blow.

The bartender's cheeks puffed out like he was a squirrel storing walnuts, his eyes bugged, and his skin turned fish-belly white. He made a croaking sound in his gullet, and then his eyes receded back into his head and rolled up into his skull.

Clint dropped him like a dead snake. He reached into his jeans, pulled out a handful of change and slammed it on the bar.

"Guess I'm going to have to tend the bar myself," he announced to the stunned crowd.

Before anyone could think to protest, Clint hopped over the bar and uncorked a bottle of beer. He poured it foaming into a glass, emptied it, and opened another.

The man who'd started to protest leaned over the bar and said, "Mister, I don't know who you are, but you sure laid Eli out cold. Mr. Mooney comes back, he's going to be pretty upset about not having a bartender."

"He own this place?" Clint asked.

"That's right."

Clint licked beer foam from his lips. "Well, he serves pretty good beer, doesn't he. Maybe I'll just apply for that fella's job. Don't seem to me that he was doing all that well by the customers."

Clint looked around the room. He was fully aware that some bartenders were very popular among their clientele and if Eli was one of them, there might be trouble. But there wasn't.

"I'll have another whiskey," a cowboy down at the end of the bar called with a grin.

"Me too," said his friend.

"Coming right up!"

Clint grabbed two shot glasses, wiped them to a shine with a bar rag, then stepped over the unconscious bartender and marched down to the cowboys. "Here you go," he said, filling the glasses to their rims without spilling a drop.

The cowboys exchanged grins. One said, "Mister, you sure give a man the full measure."

"I try," Clint said.

"Hey, mister," another man called, "I want to see if you can pour us drinks like that without spilling any."

Clint did. And he kept on pouring for two more hours until a tall, handsome man in his mid-thirties pushed through the batwing doors. He was dressed in a gray, pin-striped suit, with white shirt, starched collar, a gold watch and chain and a twenty-dollar derby on his head. It was clear that he had money.

"Who are you?" he demanded.

"My name is Clint."

"Well where the hell is Eli?"

Clint looked down at the floor behind the bar. "He's taking a little rest."

The man's cheeks reddened. "What the hell is going on here!"

"Mr. Mooney," a cowboy began, "Eli got pretty sassy with this Clint fella and he sort of got his comeuppance."

Mooney shot an angry glance and was about to say something to the Gunsmith when several other customers chimed in to defend Clint.

"He had it comin'," a big miner with a black eye said. "Yes sir, he sure did. And this fella here pours whiskey like it was what he was born to do. He's a hell of a pourer, Mr. Mooney."

Mooney scowled. Clint judged him for a dandy, but there was nothing foppish about the man. He looked like he was in good shape, too: about six-foot one and well-proportioned. With his looks, dress and money, Clint didn't doubt for a moment that he was quite a ladies' man.

"Pour me one," Mooney demanded.

Clint smiled and poured. Didn't spill a drop and that made everyone hoot with appreciation.

"See what we mean, Mr. Mooney!" a cowboy called out. "That man can really *pour*!"

Mooney tossed his whiskey down neat. He measured Clint. He was taller by an inch or two and younger by a couple of years. He was even better looking than Clint but he didn't have the same look of danger in his eye and that kept him civil.

"You a bartender?" Mooney asked in a rough voice.

"I am many things," Clint told the man. "Bartender, gambler, gunsmith."

"You look like a man who's down on all three," Mooney said caustically.

Clint held his tongue. He did not like this self-important peacock, but he needed a job in the worst way. Even more for his poor horse than for himself.

"I could use the job."

"What about cleaning my spitoons?" Mooney asked with a cold grin. He drew a long, expensive cigar from his coat pocket and shoved it between nearly perfect and very white teeth. "You need a job that bad?"

Clint's impulse was to double up his fist and drive that big cigar right down the man's windpipe. That would change the sonofabitch's tune.

Instead, he shook his head and started to move out from around the bar. "Nope, I sure as hell don't."

"Hold it," Mooney said, raising his hand, then coming over to lean close so that his words wouldn't be heard by anyone but Clint. "I pay ten dollars a week and you get to keep all your own tips. They can be more than your wages."

"Sounds good to me."

"Yeah," Mooney said, "I thought it might. But if I or one of my boys catches you holding out money on me . . . we'll break your fucking neck. Is that understood?"

Clint's cheeks burned with anger and humiliation, but he nodded his head.

Mooney stepped back. "Then you're hired, Clint. You'll work noon 'til closing time shift six days a week. Any problems with that?"

"No."

"Then congratulations."

Mooney stuck out his hand. It was soft as that of a woman but Clint's hand wasn't exactly covered with callouses either. Mooney grinned around his cigar and tried to crush the Gunsmith's hand in his own grip. Failing that, he attempted to roll Clint's knuckles but didn't have any luck at that either.

"I don't like you much," Mooney said, puffing smoke in Clint's face.

"I don't like you either," Clint said. "But you need a bartender and I need a job."

"Then get back behind the bar."

Clint did as he was told but took his own sweet time. It gave him no pleasure to work for Mooney, but until he found something better to do, he'd stick. Besides, though he wasn't going to say anything to the owner, his tips were already in excess of three dollars. At that rate, and if his luck changed at cards, he'd have his fifty dollars for doctoring his horse in just a few days. After that and a little extra for a room and meals, he could get just as picky about work as he wanted.

Mooney stayed around about an hour, then said something about getting back to work at his law office.

"By the way, can you play that piano over there?"

Clint glanced across the room. There was a battered old piano and a little raised platform. "I cannot play a note."

"Damn," Mooney swore. "I got an old man that plays for a dollar a night and drinks. But he ain't worth a damn.

He gets drunk before ten and starts singing along with Rosie."

"Rosie?"

"Yeah. She's one of Lucy's girls. Comes over here every night and sings a few songs. It's good for my business because the customers seem to get real thirsty just watching her. Good for Miss Mullane's whorehouse too."

"Makes sense to me."

"Well, the thing of it is," Mooney said, "up until last night I've had no trouble. But last night some drunken sonofabitch grabbed Rosie and tore the front of her dress right down to her belly button."

Mooney winked. "You see, Rosie has her curves in all the right places. She's the kind of woman that brings out the very devil in a man."

Clint said nothing. He wondered what this man was getting to next.

"Anyway," Mooney said, "I want you to sort of watch out for the men. Keep 'em off Rosie."

"That doesn't sound like a bartender's job to me."

"It is if I say it is."

"All right. I'll make sure that Rosie leaves wearing a dress."

"Good." Mooney puffed rapidly on his cigar. "Of course, after she leaves here, I don't give a damn if they all rape her in the street. Just keep things orderly in my saloon."

Clint could barely nod his head. What a bastard this man was!

Stay calm, the Gunsmith told himself. A few days and nights, and you'll have enough money to quit.

THREE

Clint didn't mind pouring whiskey at the Ace High Saloon. The crowd was rough, but within an hour, a young man in his twenties with a Texas twang in his voice stared at him with amazement, and said, "Why, aren't you the Gunsmith!"

Clint didn't enjoy his reputation as a fast gun. In fact, he never even brought up the subject, though he wouldn't lie about his past years as a lawman and occasional bounty hunter.

"I am by trade a gunsmith," he admitted, polishing a glass.

"The hell you are!" The man looked up and down the bar and his voice became excited. "Don't you fellas know who this *really* is! This is Clint Adams! The Gunsmith! All of you have heard of him."

Conversation along the bar stopped. Clint sighed with resignation but kept on polishing the glasses.

"So what the hell are you doing behind the bar!" the young cowboy exclaimed. "You're famous!"

Clint sighed. "I'm also tired, dirty, hungry, and broke right now. You have to understand that a man can't eat off his past accomplishments."

The Texan just stared at him in disbelief. "Why, I saw you face off against the Santana brothers down in El Paso. They were quicker than rattlers. You beat 'em both! I was in the Wild Dog Saloon when you braced them and the bullets started flying! I remember that one of them winged you across the arm. You were bleeding real bad."

"It wasn't that bad," Clint said. "But yeah, it was close and they were pretty quick."

" 'Pretty quick!' " The man turned to the saloon full of men. "The Gunsmith says the Santana Brothers were just 'pretty quick.' Hell, before he arrived to take them on, they'd killed two sheriffs, a United States Marshal and a some of the best men in Texas. But this man—the Gunsmith—well boys, he's the fastest hombre ever to slap leather."

Clint colored with embarrassment. "I'd just as soon leave my gun in its holster and live in peace," he told everyone. "I'm just trying to earn beans and a bed."

The Texan's face grew somber. "Well sir, I can understand that myself. Yes sir, things are hard these days. Seems to me though, that a man with your special talents ought to be able to . . ."

"What are you drinking this evening?" Clint asked bluntly.

"Why . . . why whiskey, of course." The Texan frowned. "Did I say something wrong, Mr. Adams?"

"Nope," Clint said. "It's just that my 'special talents,' as you put it, are kind of deadly and I only use them as a last resort. I see no good that comes from bragging about how many men I've killed."

The Texan looked ashamed. "I can understand that." He leaned closer to the Gunsmith. "I got a few dollars if you need a loan."

Clint's anger vanished. "Naw," he said, "I'm fine. Just had a run of bad luck. It comes to all of us now and then."

"I'll say it does," the Texan admitted. "Why, I broke my leg eight weeks ago and I've had some money problems myself. You see, I'm a bronc buster. One of the best. But a man has got to be sound to do it."

"He sure does," Clint said agreeably.

During the next hour while he poured drinks, Clint listened to the Texan pour out his own tale of woe. His name was Willie Walton and he'd been born and raised down around the Big Bend country of Texas. He was Clint's height, just under six foot, lean and free with his smiles and his money considering that he'd not been able to ride the bad horses and earn his living. To make matters worse, Willie's mother had recently died and his girlfriend down in Laredo had dumped him for a wealthy young rancher.

"Bad luck runs in streaks," Clint commiserated.

"It sure does." The Texan had been drinking steadily and his eyes were a little glazed and unfocused as he stared at Clint. "But it raises my poor spirits to see that one so famous as yourself can also fall on hard times. Makes me realize I ain't the only one that fate has pissed upon."

Clint was about to suggest that Willie quit drinking and get a good night's rest when a short woman with black hair, bold brown eyes and a low-cut blue velvet dress sashayed into the saloon.

"Hi boys!" she called.

Everyone in the place returned her greeting and Clint could see from their faces that they not only lusted for the woman, but they also genuinely liked her.

"Man oh man," Willie breathed, "ain't she something!"

"Yep," Clint said, "she is an eyeful."

"They say that Rosie only sleeps with Mr. Mooney and that once in a while she goes down to Tucson or Prescott and pleasures their rich men. Just three days ago, I was here when some of the boys offered her fifty dollars to go upstairs to a room after they drawed straws for a winner. Rosie said she wouldn't for a hundred dollars."

Clint didn't believe it. He'd seen hundreds like Rosie, though few quite as pretty. "She's living on borrowed time," he said. "In a few years, her looks will be gone and she'll be faded just like all the girls that went before her."

Willie groaned. "I sure hope you're wrong. Rosie is one of the reasons I'm sticking around this one-horse town.

Sometimes, she lets me buy her a drink or two before she sings. Say, I'll introduce you to her."

Before Clint could say anything, Willie lurched forward, and when he came to Rosie he leaned forward and whispered something in her ear. She laughed and then looked at Clint.

The Gunsmith took a deep breath. Rosie was quite a woman all right. Her eyes could burn a hole through a man and turn his thoughts from his work. Clint forced his eyes down to the glass in his hand and he polished it furiously.

"Hey, Gunsmith!" Willie called, leading the woman over to the bar. "I want you to meet Miss Rosie!"

"Hello, Miss Rosie," Clint said, meeting her bold eyes and trying to keep them above her neckline. She was younger than he'd first thought. Maybe under twenty. Without the heavy makeup she used, she'd have been even prettier.

"So what's a famous gunman like you doing working behind the bar?" she asked, her voice low and throaty.

"Making a living. What's a pretty young girl like you doing in a place like this?"

She laughed. "I'm doing the same."

"Can I buy you both a drink?" Willie asked, trying to push in between them.

"No thanks," Clint said.

"Sure," Rosie said, her dark eyes locked with Clint's lighter ones.

"Well by damned," Willie said, "I guess I already spent all my money!"

The Texan looked so embarrassed that Clint paid for drinks himself. Rosie downed hers neat.

"Thanks, Clint," she said. "Mr. Mooney tells me that you've orders to keep the animals off me when I sing."

"That's right."

"Then why don't you come over and stand at my side? A lot could happen before you could get around this bartop."

Willie cleared his throat. "I'll stay by your side," he offered. "My friend Clint has to tend this bar."

Rosie reached up and patted Willie's cheek. "You are a sweetheart, but maybe it would be better if you tended bar and the Gunsmith spared a little of his precious time to see that no one lays a hand on me tonight."

Willie didn't like that suggestion one damned bit, even though it made sense. He was half drunk and obviously possessive, and Clint could see that young Texan might act foolishly and get himself into big trouble.

"Are you ready to sing?" Clint asked.

"I sure am."

"Willie, pour 'em," Clint said, moving around the bar and leading the dance hall girl over to the little raised stage beside the old piano.

The piano player wouldn't sit down until Willie brought him three mugs of beer. He gulped down two and chirped, "What shall we start with, Miss Rosie?"

"Let's do, 'The Girl from St. Louis,' " Rosie said, hopping up on the stage as the piano player began to pound the keys.

Clint stood off to one side and he had to smile as Rosie sang a bawdy song about a girl from St. Louis who worked her way up and down the Mississippi River falling in and out of love with riverboat gamblers.

Cutting into the thunderous applause, Rosie began to sing a slow, heart-rending ballad about a girl from Virginia City whose husband died in the mines and had been forced to sell herself in order to eat. The song was maudlin, but Rosie sang it very well, and when she finished there were tears on the cheeks of many strong men.

"Sing 'Sweet Betsy from Pike'!" a man yelled.

Rosie nodded to the piano player, who missed as many notes as he made, and soon had everyone stomping, clapping his hands and singing along to Rosie's rousing rendition of the popular song. Clint himself was grinning and clapping his hands. But suddenly the words died on Rosie's lips and the music stopped.

Clint saw the woman's eyes widen with alarm, and he

turned to see a huge, bearded man filling the doorway. The man was at least six foot six and three hundred pounds. The crowd parted when he came swaggering across the saloon and stopped before the singer.

"I guess you're through singing," he rumbled. "And I'm tired of waiting."

He started to reach out for Rosie, but Clint moved at the same instant, his hand going to the gun on his hip. It came up in one swift, smooth motion, and he cocked it right in the giant's ear.

"Mister, I don't know who you are, but you're on your way out of this saloon."

The giant turned to glare at the Gunsmith. He was ugly and his face was covered with scars. His nose was surprisingly small. It had been fist-busted and was misshapen. His eyes were set far back under a shelf of bone and brow. Clint had seen more compassionate eyes in the face of a badger.

"Put the gun down," the giant said, "or I'll shove it up your ass and pull the trigger."

"You're either crazy or wanting to die," Clint said. "When I pull iron, I never bluff. So what's it to be? What little brains you got scattered all over the floor, or are you getting out of here right now?"

"Elmer?" the giant said.

Clint heard the unmistakable sound of a double-barreled shotgun being cocked. Out of the corner of his eye he saw another huge figure who had entered the saloon.

"Your brother?"

"Yep. And he don't give a damn about shit. He'll open up with both barrels."

"That scatter gun will take your head off the same as it will mine," Clint said.

"Don't matter to me."

Clint blinked. He looked straight into those black eyes and knew the man was telling him the God's honest truth. In all of Clint's years as a lawman, he'd met hard men of all types but only one or two who'd been absolutely without any fear of death. Apparently, this giant and his brother were of that mold.

"What the hell do you want?" Clint said, his finger hard on his trigger and the barrel of his gun right next to the giant's temple.

"We want her!"

"No."

"Elmer? Cut loose on us."

It was crazy. It was insane but Clint knew that it was going to happen. He was going to be killed, Rosie was going to be killed, and so was this giant, along with anyone else in the path of Elmer's shotgun blast.

Clint did the only thing he could do. He swung his sixgun around and fired at Elmer just as fast as he could pull the trigger. Elmer took Clint's first slug in the forehead and another through the right cheek. His shotgun erupted with both barrels into the ceiling and blew a crystal chandelier right through the roof.

Everyone dove for cover. Rosie screamed. Clint tried to swing his sixgun back on the giant but the man whipped his elbow into Clint's side and knocked him flying halfway across the saloon.

The Gunsmith crashed over a table, but somehow Clint held onto his gun, and when the giant reached for his own sidearm Clint shot him in the chest. The giant batted at the crimson rose on his shirtfront and lurched forward, eyes mad with hatred, hands outstretched and bent on breaking Clint's neck.

Clint had only two more bullets in his gun and he wasn't sure that they were enough to save his life. So he took aim and shot the giant right between the eyes.

"Ahhhh!" the man bellowed, grabbing his face and taking two more steps before crashing to the floor.

For almost a full minute, no one spoke or even moved. Then, Rosie jumped off the stage, threw herself at Clint, and began to sob in his arms.

"It's all right," he said. "They're dead. It's over."

Willie Watson shouted, "Drinks on the house! Drinks on the house!"

As if waking up from a sleep, the patrons of the Ace High Saloon surged forward, cheering and shouting.

Clint shook his head and stared at the dead giant. "Who were they?"

"They were mountain men," Rosie said. "They came down just last week. They scared everyone to death. They never even told anyone their names."

Clint swallowed. "I better get back to work," he said. "Willie is bound to pour the place dry and I'll lose my job."

"To hell with this lousy job," Rosie breathed. "You saved my life just now. I've got enough money for the both of us and I need a man to hold me tonight. Interested?"

"My horse is lame. I need fifty dollars. After that . . ."

She shoved a hand down the front of her low cut dress and yanked out a wad of bills. "Keep it. I'll earn that much in one night when I work."

"Not from me you won't," Clint told her.

She touched his face. "Mister, with you, it won't be work."

He hesitated.

"What's wrong?" she asked. "You must like me or you wouldn't have saved my life."

"Oh," he said as someone shoved a bottle into his fist. "I like you just fine. I think I'd like you even better after spending the night in your bed."

"Well then?"

"Willie thinks he's in love with you. And I sort of like the guy and don't want to hurt his feelings."

"He's a man. He'll understand how it is. Besides, you're the one that saved my life, not Willie."

She ran her hand down the front of his pants. "I don't ask twice."

Clint took a deep breath. "All right," he said, feeling his

manhood thicken and rise. "Let's get out of here."

Outside, Clint untied Duke from the hitching rail and then he and Rosie led the horse down to the livery.

"He sure is lame," Rosie said. "Beautiful horse. Is he going to get well?"

"You bet," Clint said. "He just needs some rest and good attention."

"He'll get it here," Rosie said. "I don't own a horse, but everyone says Hector has a way with animals."

"I'm counting on that," the Gunsmith said.

Hector showed up a few minutes later and when Clint waved fifty dollars in front of his face, the liveryman turned all smiles.

"You just don't worry about a thing. Come by as often as you like. I'll have this big sonofabitch dancing for you in two weeks."

Clint left Duke feeling confident that the gelding was in good hands.

"Where are we going now?" he asked, taking Rosie's arm.

"Over to Miss Lucy's Place. I've got the best upstairs room in the house—next to her own."

"Oh," Clint said, taking a deep breath and chuckling.

"What's so funny?"

"I was just thinking how angry lawyer Mooney will be when he finds out that Willie has given away all his whiskey."

Rosie chuckled. "Mooney is a tight-fisted bastard. He's plenty rich enough to cover the loss. I just hope that he doesn't take it out on Willie."

Clint stopped with alarm. "He'd do that? Over a few bottles of cheap whiskey?"

"Naw, probably not."

"If he does," Clint warned, "Mooney will have to answer to me."

Rosie kissed his cheek and pulled him after her as they continued on to Miss Lucy's Place.

The first one they saw inside was Annabelle. She pouted, noting the way that Rosie held on to the Gunsmith's arm. "Say, you were supposed to ask for me."

"He's mine," Rosie said. "Go find your own."

The inside of Miss Lucy's Place was fixed up real nice, with red velvet wallpaper and curtains. At one end of the room was a polished bar as fine as any on the Comstock and behind it was a big nude hanging in a gilded frame. She was eating an apple and a white dog was staring at her with its tongue hanging out.

"You like that picture?" Rosie asked as they started upstairs.

"Yeah," Clint said.

"Me too. Especially the dog. I bet his tongue ain't hanging out because of that apple."

Rosie giggled wickedly and Clint hurried after up the stairs knowing that he was in for a real good time.

FOUR

"Nice," Clint said as Rosie closed and locked the door behind her. "Real nice."

"Thank you," she said, turning around to discover that he was admiring her rather than the room.

Rosie smiled and evaded Clint's grasp to move over to a small bar. "Would you like a glass of champagne?"

"Sure." Clint dropped his hands to his sides. A lot of women, and he figured Rosie was one of them, preferred to be romanced before lovemaking. Well, Clint thought, I'm in no rush. "I could sure use a bath."

"That can be arranged," Rosie said, unlocking the door and disappearing for a few minutes. She returned to pour them both glasses of champagne. "Hot bathwater will be here in about two minutes."

"To us," Clint said, offering a toast.

"To my hero," she said, clinking her glass as his own. "So, how many men have you killed, Gunsmith?"

Clint's smile faded. He tossed down his drink and said, "I've never kept track but the answer has always been the same as it was since the first—too damn many."

Rosie glanced at the well-used gun resting on his hip, then she gulped her champagne and walked over to a little antique end table where she picked up a daguerrotype. "This was my mother." Clint saw a remarkable resemblance between the mother and her daughter. They both had

25

the same heart-shaped face, wide-spaced eyes and pretty mouths. "She was very lovely," Clint said. "Just like you."

"She was raised in North Carolina, the only child of a wealthy Southern plantation owner," Rosie said. "When the Union Army came through, they shot my grandparents for trying to stop them from running off all the livestock. My mother was seventeen and they chased her into the fields and . . . and had their way with her."

Rosie refilled her glass. "Mother lost consciousness after a while. Nine months later, I was born out of wedlock."

Clint nodded, his mouth crimping down at the corners. He could hear the pain in Rosie's voice and knew that, despite her front, she was ashamed.

"It wasn't your mother's fault," Clint said. "And it has nothing to do with you."

"Hasn't it?"

"No."

"I was conceived in lust and I am by nature a lusting woman."

"You are a good woman," he said emphatically. "I could tell that when you sang to the saloon crowd."

"You're very kind," she said with a smile of gratitude. "I knew that from the start. You're not anything like a famous gunman. You're too nice."

Rosie kissed his mouth. Her lips fired the Gunsmith's blood. He felt her heart pound against his chest and her breath came faster. Clint reached up behind Rosie and began to unbutton her dress. He was doing a pretty good job of it when a knock sounded at the door and the familiar voice of Mr. Washington called, "Your bath water is ready, Miss Rosie."

Clint not longer gave a damn about a bath but Rosie hurried to open the door. Mr. Washington grinned. "I could shore use some help, sir."

"Sure," Clint said, going out in the hall to help carry in steaming buckets of water.

They soon had Miss Rosie's big tin bathtub filled. She

tipped the black man with a whole dollar and he left, but not before he gave Clint a wink and said, "You have yoself a real good time, now. Anything you need, you jest call Mr. Washington. Hear now?"

"We'll do that," Clint said, suppressing a grin of his own.

When the door closed, Clint said, "That old black gentleman seems to keep real busy around here."

"He enjoys himself."

"I'll bet," Clint deadpanned.

Rosie began to undress and Clint said, "You coming in too?"

"Sure. Why not?"

Clint couldn't think of a single good reason, and when Rosie stood naked before him he was more than happy to have her jump into the bathtub. She had a lush body, with high, firm breasts, a hard, flat belly, and short but shapely legs. Just watching her gave Clint a big, throbbing erection.

"As you can see, I'm not too sure that I'm going to be able to concentrate on getting clean."

Rosie licked her red lips. "You first, big boy."

Clint stepped into the tub. "Ouch! Damn it's hot!" he complained, easing slowly into the water.

"You'll get used to it in a minute," Rosie said before climbing in on top of him and leaning forward to kiss his mouth.

"Here," she whispered, cupping one of her breasts to his mouth. Clint sighed with contentment as he leaned back and used his teeth and tongue to fire her passion. After a few minutes, Rosie was spreading herself open and reaching for him. Clint groaned with satisfaction as the girl slowly impaled herself on his throbbing manhood.

"Lean forward," she breathed into his ear.

"Huh?"

"Lean forward and I'll wash your back."

"Later," he told her, as his hands pushed down hard on

her hips and he drove himself into her eager body.

Rosie began to move up and down on him—slowly at first, then faster and faster until they were spilling water onto the floor.

"Oh," she breathed, "you feel wonderful!"

"You don't feel too bad yourself," he said, driving his rod in and out and gripping her firm buttocks, all the while sucking on her bouncing breasts.

Rosie was going wild. Her eyes rolled up in her head and she was bucking like a filly being ridden for the very first time. Huge waves were breaking over the tin tub and soaking her nice rugs but neither one of them gave a damn.

Clint was wondering how much longer he could hang on when Rosie suddenly threw back her head and cried out in ecstasy. "Oh, yes, my darling, yes!"

The Gunsmith growled way down in his throat and his seed pumped through his plunging rod to fill her womanhood. Rosie's body milked him powerfully until she collapsed forward against his chest, trying to catch her breath.

At last, she said, "I'm going to have to ask Mr. Washington to bring up some more bath water."

"Naw," Clint said, "we can make do."

Still panting, Rosie managed to nod her head. "Now will you lean forward so I can wash your back?"

"Sure."

Rosie washed him from head to toe and when she was finished, the bath was a little muddy.

"Thanks," he said when she handed him a bath towel. "I really needed that."

"The bath?"

"Yeah, and the other."

"Been a long time?"

"Couple of weeks."

She dressed in a pair of blue jeans and a soft cotton shirt that Rosie didn't trouble herself to button. She looked like a school girl, happy and satisfied.

"How old are you?" he asked.

"Old enough to satisfy a man like you," she replied. "And old enough to make my own way in life."

Clint surveyed the room. It was beautifully decorated, and although he wasn't any expert on furniture there were some antique and European pieces that were obviously valuable. The soaked rugs were also expensive as were the pictures on the walls, the satin curtains, and the hand-carved, four-poster bed he would soon have the pleasure of testing.

"Is all this furniture yours?"

"I wish it was," Rosie said. "But it belongs to Miss Lucy. If you think *this* room is nice, you should see *her* room."

"Miss Lucy must think a lot of you."

Rosie nodded. "She's like my big sister. And she knows I'd never bring anyone up here who would get drunk and smash furniture or try to steal these beautiful paintings."

"Have you known her long?"

"About four years. When I arrived in this town, I owned nothing except the dress I was wearing and an old satchel filled with rags. Miss Lucy took me in as a cook and maid. I was never one of her girls until I decided that I wanted to be."

"Why?"

"The money, of course. Miss Lucy made it clear right from the start that I should only have her special clients."

"Meaning those with lots of money and expensive tastes. The kind of men who can afford the best."

Rosie nodded. "That's right. You've got it figured out."

"Let me take another guess," Clint said. "One of your most important 'special clients' is lawyer James Mooney."

Her smile died. "Yes," she said bitterly. "He'd like to have me all to himself, but I couldn't stand that. He gets crazy jealous."

"Then he's going to really hate my guts when he finds out that I not only left my bartending job in Willie Watson's liberal hands, but that I came here and made love to his girl."

Rosie opened a second bottle of champagne and poured herself another glass. She was, Clint noticed, a pretty hard drinker.

"I have to be honest with you, Gunsmith."

"Call me Clint."

"All right, Clint. When Jim discovers what you've done, he's going to go wild. He'll come here and raise hell. He may even try and punish me."

"He won't lay a hand on you," Clint vowed. "Not as long as I'm around."

"Yes," Rosie said, "that's the problem—you can't be around all the time."

Clint saw that the girl was really scared and it occurred to him that her fear was the reason she was tossing the champagne down so fast.

"Say," he said, "if Mooney comes over here, I'll just tell him that you're my girl now and he's out of the picture. I'll let him know that it's over."

"You will?"

"Sure." Clint took the bottle from her hand and placed it on the table. He drew her over to the bed, eased her down on it, and lay beside her. Kissing her face, he said, "The man doesn't own you, Rosie. You're free to tell him to go to hell."

"I really want to," she said, hugging his neck. "He scares me. He makes me do awful things when we're up here alone together. Things that make me feel like an animal instead of a human being. He makes me . . ."

Clint put his finger over her lips. "Whatever he makes you do is in the past. I quit him, so have you."

"Will you take me with you when you leave Quartz?"

He hesitated but then realized that he'd gotten this girl into a fix and her safety was his responsibility now. The least he owed her was a fresh start in a big town where she might be able to shake her past and find respectability.

"I'll take you. But my horse is lame and I won't be leaving for a couple of weeks."

"That long!"

He saw panic in her large brown eyes. "Take it easy," he soothed. "I promise you'll be safe."

She kissed him passionately. "Clint, I've got lots of money hidden away. Over a thousand dollars! You could buy us a couple of sound horses and we could run away tonight!"

She looked so eager and excited that it wasn't easy for Clint to shake his head and say, "I can't."

"But why not!"

"It's my horse," he told her, knowing how ridiculous that sounded to this frightened girl. "You see, that gelding and I have been through a lot of close scrapes."

"But . . ."

"I just can't leave a horse that's saved my life," he said flatly. "But in the meantime, I'll have a little heart-to-heart talk with lawyer Mooney."

Rosie was about to say something but a loud hammering on her door interrupted.

"Rosie, open this door!"

She paled. "It's him!"

Clint slipped off the bed and buttoned up the front of his pants before he slipped his gun from its holster and went to the door.

"What do you want?"

"Gunsmith, you're in deep trouble!"

Clint unlocked the door to find Mooney shaking with anger and gripping a Colt which he looked wild enough to draw from his holster if provoked any further.

"Get your hands away from that gun," Clint warned. "You wouldn't stand a chance against me."

"You sonofabitch!" Mooney cursed, looking over the Gunsmith's shoulder to the bed. "I told you to *protect*, not *fuck* her!"

Clint grabbed the lawyer by the lapels of his tailored suit jacket and threw him across the hall to slam against the wall.

"Let me make this very clear," Clint said. "You don't own Rosie. You never did. And she doesn't want to see you again. Do you understand that!"

When Mooney cursed, the Gunsmith drove his fist into the side of the man's jaw. Mooney slid down the wall and Clint knelt before him.

He grabbed the attorney by his expensive silk tie and said, "If you bother her again, or send anyone else to get or harm her, I'll hold you personally responsible. If she has an 'accident' I'll make you wish you were never born. Is that understood?"

The attorney made a strangling sound, and Clint gave the man the benefit of the doubt. He said, "Find yourself another lovebird, Mooney. This one has flown your coop."

Clint slammed the door behind him and Rosie threw herself into his arms. "Thank you!"

"You're welcome," he said, hearing Mooney's heavy thudding footsteps recede down the hallway.

"Do you think he'll behave now?" Clint asked.

"I don't know," she answered, pulling him toward the bed, "but I wish to heaven we were leaving Quartz tonight and never coming back."

Clint kind of wished the same, though he would never have admitted it. And he might even have considered leaving Duke in this town to heal and taking Rosie to safety except for Mooney. The lawyer was just the kind of man who'd kill an innocent horse out of some kind of twisted revenge.

"Everything will be fine now," Clint said with an assurance that he did not feel inside.

That night they not only locked Rosie's door but dragged a heavy piece of furniture behind it for added protection from Mooney or anyone he might hire. They made passionate love again and again, and then they slept until noon when they were awakened by a firm knock on the door.

Clint grabbed his pistol. "Who is it?"

"It's Lucy Mullane and we need to have a long talk."

"Coming!" Rosie jumped out of bed and Clint followed, knuckling sleep from his eyes. Rosie had nearly screwed his brains out last night, and he felt thick-headed and more exhausted than when he'd first limped into this town.

When they dragged the furniture away and unlocked the door, they opened it to see Miss Lucy standing before them with a black eye.

"Oh my God!" Rosie cried. "What happened!"

The beautiful madam pushed inside the room and locked the door behind her before she said, "I was attacked last night."

"By Mooney," Clint asked, feeling his blood start to boil.

"No," she said, "of course not. He's far too clever to act that stupid. But it was a warning from him."

Clint swore under his breath, then suddenly remembered that he was naked.

"I'll go see him," Clint said.

"If you do," Lucy told him, "you'll be walking right into his trap and you'll never come back alive."

"How many men does he have?"

"As many as it takes."

Clint reached for his pants. "I'll figure out some way to get to him."

But Lucy Mullane grabbed his arm. "You can't," she said.

"And why the hell not!"

"Because."

Clint waited for an explanation. When it didn't come, he said, "That's no answer. I'm going after him."

"He's my husband!" Lucy said.

"What!" Rosie cried, hand flying to her mouth.

Lucy seemed to deflate. "I guess I had better explain all of it. But it will take some time."

Clint pulled on his pants and growled. "I could sure use some coffee first."

Lucy called for Mr. Washington. The man must have been waiting because he showed up a minute later. After the madam made her request for a pot of coffee and three cups, the old black man disappeared only to return before Clint could button his shirt and pull on his boots.

"I'm not sure that I can make you understand why I married James Mooney, but I'll try."

Rosie seemed dazed. "If he's your husband, why . . ."

"Did I allow him to use you?"

Rosie nodded.

"Because he owns this house. This furniture and everything including my soul."

Clint blinked. He reached for the coffee, deciding that whatever Miss Lucy was about to say was going to require a clear head to understand.

"Did you ever hear," Miss Lucy began, "of a famous outlaw and hired killer named Ben Towers?"

"I've heard of him," Clint said.

"So have I," Rosie said with confusion in her dark eyes, "but what . . ."

"I had his baby six years ago when I was living in Kansas," Lucy told them. "Ben took my baby away by force and I've never seen her since. I made the mistake of telling this to Mooney who made some inquiries. He says he's found her and she's living with foster parents who don't love her."

The madam sniffled. "I agreed to do anything to find out where my daughter was living so that I could have her back after all these years. But I forgot that the courts would not look too favorably on that, given my profession."

Clint suddenly understood. "And lawyer Mooney would make sure that the courts understood your profession."

"Yes. So he demanded payment. My body was enough at first, then he wanted more in return for the promise to deliver my child—no questions asked."

"But of course, he never did," Clint said.

"No, but I foolishly gave him everything he wanted. I

was desperate. I wasn't thinking clearly. I even gave him you, Rosie!"

The madam covered her face and wept bitterly. Clint reached for his holster and sixgun.

"Before I go, is there any reason why I can't trade Mooney his worthless life in return for your daughter and his silence?"

Lucy looked up at him with tears streaming down her face. "Ben Towers is still alive! And he will kill her if anything happens to Mooney! That's the hold he's got over me! Can't you see how horrible the man is now!"

Clint took a deep breath. "I thought Towers was killed in an attempted prison breakout down in Yuma."

"Oh how I wish he had been!" Lucy cried. "But he's alive. Mooney supports him for no other reason than to keep his hold over me."

Clint began to pace back and forth. His head still throbbed, but the weariness was gone, and his mind was racing.

"I have to find your daughter, then take care of Ben Towers. Any idea where he might be found?"

Rosie shook her head. "No. Only I heard that he was salting mines for Mooney somewhere in Colorado."

"Salting mines?"

The madam nodded her head. "That's right. It's a scheme of some kind they're working. I don't know anything about it and I don't care. All I want is my child returned."

"I'll find Ben Towers," Clint promised.

"I want to go with you," Rosie pleaded. "Please don't leave me in this town!"

"All right," Clint said. He inspected the madam's eye. "Are you going to be safe here, or do you want to come along with us?"

"I had better stay. If both Rosie and I left . . . Mooney might order Ben to kill my little girl before you could find and stop him."

"What's her name?"

"Lisa. She's just six years old now."

"Do you have a picture of her?" Clint asked. "Something that would help us identify the child?"

"She has a birthmark on her right forearm."

It wasn't much to go on. A long-missing child. A professional killer who was supposed to be dead and was instead salting gold mines somewhere in Colorado. It wasn't much at all. But looking into the faces of these two women, Clint knew that he had to find Ben Towers, make him tell where the girl was to be found, and then kill the man.

And after all that, he'd return to this town and settle the score with Mooney. Settle it for keeps.

FIVE

"Before you go," Lucy Mullane said, "I think I ought to tell you that Mooney will probably have this house watched. But perhaps I could still have you and Rosie smuggled out in my carriage and . . ."

"No," Clint said. "I'm not leaving without my horse. He's lame, but I'll lead him on over to Prescott."

"Are you sure?"

Clint remembered the hatred in Mooney's eyes. "Yep. It won't be easy on Duke, but at least I know that he'll be safe."

"Then you'll just have to take your chances," Lucy said as she handed the Gunsmith a thick envelope.

"What's this?"

"Money," she said. "Enough money for fresh horses, supplies and whatever else you might need to find and return my child."

Clint stuffed it into his coat pocket. "Thanks."

"If you find my daughter," Lucy said, "don't bring her here. Just send me a telegram and I'll come for her. I don't want her to know what I do for a living."

"So you'll just leave all this behind?"

"It doesn't really belong to me anymore. Remember?"

Clint nodded. He would honor this lady's wishes, but he would not consider his work done until he had finally brought lawyer Mooney down.

"Take care of yourself," he said.

"Same to you," Lucy told him. "And watch your back trail. I expect Mooney will send men after you because of what you did to him last night."

"I expect," Clint said.

He turned to Rosie. "You wait here until I come back with the horses. No sense in you putting yourself in any more danger than is necessary."

Rosie didn't want to let him go alone, but Clint overrode her objections. If Mooney had hired an ambusher or had gunmen waiting for him, having Rosie safe indoors made good sense.

Clint checked his gun before he said goodbye. Then Rosie hugged his neck, and every one of the other girls who worked at Lucy's Place kissed and hugged him too.

"I never been in such pretty company," he told all those women just before he straightened his hat and headed out the door.

The sun was shining brightly, and Clint pulled the brim of his black Stetson down low over his eyes. He wasn't sure what to expect and even had his doubts that Mooney would actually try to have him ambushed on Quartz's main street.

He made it to the livery without incident. In fact, he didn't even seem to attract his usual amount of attention. Several tough-looking men watched him from the boardwalk, but none of them gave any indication they were Mooney's hired guns looking for an opening to draw their guns.

The liveryman was doctoring Duke's hoof when Clint walked into his barn. The Gunsmith came up behind the man and said, "Does that hoof look any better today?"

Hector twisted around. "It'll take a lot more time."

"I'm afraid that I don't have that anymore," Clint said. "I'm going to have to lead my horse on down to Prescott starting this afternoon."

The man dropped the hoof. "What!"

"I have no choice," Clint said, unwilling to explain fully.

"Well I ain't giving you back your fifty dollars!"

"Didn't figure to ask," Clint said. "I've decided to use it toward a pair of sound horses and an extra saddle."

The liveryman didn't look a bit pleased at this news. He argued a few minutes but when he saw that the Gunsmith's mind was set, he gave up.

"All right, then, dammit! Come along with me back to the corral and I'll show you what you can choose from."

"One of them will be for Miss Rosie," Clint said. "If it were to prove unsound, it might be real hard on her—and later on you."

The liveryman's face grew dark with anger. "Is that a threat?"

"Nope. A promise."

"Humph!" the man snorted, as he led Clint out through the back door to a big pole corral containing at least twenty horses of all ages, sizes and descriptions.

"Which ones are for sale?"

"All of 'em. Take your pick."

"Which ones are broken to ride and sound of limb?"

"All but that big roan and that pinto pony."

Clint stepped inside the corral and the horses began to mill about. The Gunsmith was a good judge of horseflesh because he'd had to be during his law career. If you went after a man with a bounty on his head, you had best have a sound horse between your legs. One with good wind, sound feet, legs and plenty of stamina.

"I like that big buckskin gelding for myself," Clint said, watching the horse carefully. "How much?"

"Fifty dollars. Best horse in the bunch. You know how to pick 'em."

"All right. And for Miss Rosie, I'll take that sorrel mare with the flaxen mane and tail."

"She's a beauty. Fast, too."

"How much?"

"Thirty and you're getting a good deal at that."

"I'll give seventy-five for the both and you'll throw in a saddle and two bridles."

"What!"

Clint slipped back outside. "Let's get them bridled and saddled," he said, heading back inside to get his own saddle.

A quarter hour later, the liveryman was still bitching about the prices, but he didn't hesitate to take Clint's money.

"You pass through this way again with a lame horse," the man said, "I hope you just keep moving."

Clint chuckled. "You've done all right, Hector. Your problem is that you want to get rich off everyone that rides into this place."

The liveryman hooted, and when Clint mounted the buckskin and the powerful gelding began to buck, he hooted even louder. The Gunsmith managed to drag the animal's head up and get it under control, but he was none too happy.

"I thought you told me that this one was the best in the corral and broke to ride!"

"He is the best and he is broke to ride. But he takes a little ironin' out."

If the Gunsmith had been wearing a pair of spurs on his bootheels, he'd have used them on the buckskin.

"This animal have any more surprises?"

"Nope."

"Then hand me the reins of the sorrel and the rope to Duke's halter," Clint ordered.

"It sure is a shame you're taking that black horse away lame like that," the liveryman groused. "I'll still buy him from you if the price is right."

"No thanks," Clint said, riding out of the barn without a backward glance. Hector might be a hell of a horse doctor, but he was not a man with whom the Gunsmith had enjoyed doing business. He was a mite too greedy.

Clint rode back up the main street leading poor Duke and the stylish little sorrel mare. When abreast of the Ace High Saloon, Willie Watson came rushing outside looking madder than hell. His eyes were bloodshot and he was unsteady on his feet.

"The word is that you're taking Miss Rosie away," Willie snarled, blocking Clint's path.

The Gunsmith reined his horse up sharply—otherwise he might have ridden over the top of Willie. "It's Rosie's choice."

"I thought you understood how I felt about her!"

"I do, Willie. You feel about her the same way as all the others when she sings. But that doesn't mean you have any right to expect her to stay in this flea-infested town."

"I think you ought to just ride the hell on out of Quartz and leave it the way it was before you came."

Clint's eyes narrowed. He leaned forward in his saddle and said, "What the hell is the matter with you anyway? Why are you crowding me so hard? Did Mooney put you up to trouble?"

"Uh-uh," Willie said, wagging his head back and forth. "Mr. Mooney ain't got nothing to do with this. It's about Miss Rosie—the girl I love!"

Clint expelled a deep sigh. The last thing he wanted was to get into a scrape with Willie.

"Why don't you step aside. I'll be back someday and if you're still of a mind, we can have a few beers and talk this out between us."

"No!" Willie cried, suddenly backing up and shading the gun on his hip. "You ain't takin' my girl!"

"Damn fool," Clint grated. "She isn't your girl! She never was. Mooney's the one that's been using her. I'm just setting her free."

But Willie wasn't listening. He had made up his mind not to let Clint take the girl of his dreams and he was determined to stop him at any cost.

"You either turn around and ride off," Willie said, fingers twitching over his gunbutt, "or you draw!"

Clint ground his teeth in frustration. He looked all around, then slowly dismounted and led his horses forward. He made himself smile. "Willie, you win."

The young cowboy stared blankly at him. "You mean that?"

"Sure." The Gunsmith extended his hand. The fury in Willie's eyes died and he grinned loosely.

But when he stuck his hand out, Clint doubled up his fist and ripped a powerful uppercut at the point of Willie's jaw. Sober, Willie might have had the reflexes to step back or block the punch, but drunk he was a wide-open target. Clint felt a shock travel all the way up his arm as his fist exploded against Willie's chin. The cowboy's eyes crossed and his knees buckled. He landed on his back and lay still.

Clint rubbed his knuckles. "I sure didn't want to do that," he said. "But maybe when you sober up and regain your senses, you'll realize I did you a favor."

The Gunsmith climbed back on his horse, and the buckskin tried to drag its head down for bucking, but Clint was ready this time, and punished the animal with his heels.

He rode around Willie Watson and on up the street until he came to Miss Lucy's Place.

Rosie came bolting out the door and threw herself onto the mare. "Let's get out of here!"

Clint was of the same mind, but with a lame horse there was nothing they could do but keep walking.

"If he sends men after us," Rosie said, "what are we going to do if we can't run?"

"We fight," Clint said. "We stand our ground and fight. Have you ever used a gun?"

"A derringer. But I'm a terrible shot at anything over ten feet away."

"I've an extra sixgun in my saddlebags," Clint said. "By the time we get to Prescott and find Duke a temporary

KILLER'S GOLD   43

home, I'll have you shooting the hairs off a squirrel's tail
at thirty yards."

They rode a few miles in silence, frequently twisting
around to check their back trail. They saw no one following them, but that didn't give Clint any great comfort.
Ambushers usually waited up ahead, and they were nearly
always crack shots and impossible to spot before they fired.

"Well," Rosie said, her mood lifting. "It looks like maybe
we are going to get out of this without any trouble."

"Maybe."

Rosie frowned. "You don't sound very sure of that."

"I'm not," Clint admitted. "I've seen a few like Mooney
before. He won't let what I did to him last night pass and
he won't be of a mind to let his girl just ride away."

"I'm *not* his girl!"

"I know that and so do you. But James Mooney doesn't."

Rosie had to nod her head. "I know," she conceded.
"And to be honest, I'm worried sick about Miss Lucy. I
wish she'd have come. I don't know why she didn't."

"My guess is that she figures I might never find Ben
Towers or her daughter and that, if she left, she might not
either. As long as she's near Mooney, she's at least got a
line to her missing daughter."

"I hate him!" Rosie swore. "He's an animal!"

"We'll bring him down," Clint vowed. "We'll find Ben
Towers and he'll lead us to Miss Mullane's little girl. And
after that, I'll come back and finish it up."

"I'm coming back too."

Clint didn't want her to come back. He was hoping that,
once they reached Prescott, Rosie might decide to stay right
there and start her new life. Hell, she'd probably attract the
attention of every bachelor in town.

"We'll just play this out one day at a time, Rosie."

"Okay. But I don't know how you expect to find Ben
Towers and that little girl."

"A man like Towers sticks out," Clint said. "And if he's
into some kind of a scheme with Mooney salting mines,

then we'll hear about it soon enough."

Rosie nodded her head but she didn't look too convinced. The truth of the matter was, Clint wasn't either. Finding Ben Towers might be like searching for a needle in a haystack.

SIX

They rode steadily that day, Clint trying to pick the trail that would be easiest on Duke and, at the same time, keep a sharp lookout for trouble. It occurred to him quite often that he was being overly cautious, but after years of being a lawman he'd developed a sort of feeling in his gut whenever trouble awaited. Besides, given Mooney's violent nature and absolute ruthlessness, it seemed a fair bet that the man would send hunters to kill him and return Rosie to Quartz.

"We'll camp up there in those rocks," Clint said. Crimson and salmon fingers of color had begun to streak across the sky, promising a brilliant sundown.

"But wouldn't it be nicer down in that meadow? More feed for the horses, too."

"Sure," Clint replied, "but that's just where anyone following would expect us to camp. Be harder for anyone to sneak up on us in those rocks. As for the horses, we'll let them graze an hour down in the meadow before we make camp."

Rosie nodded, yawned and forced a weary smile. "I sure am tired. We've got to get more sleep tonight, Clint."

"We will. Duke will nicker a warning if anything approaches."

They rode on to the meadow where they found a little stream. Clint carried a fishing line and a few hooks. It was

45

easy enough to dig a few worms out of the soft earth. They caught a half dozen speckled trout just as darkness was falling.

An hour later, they had a good camp up in the rocks. It was high and well protected. The Gunsmith had built a fire under an overhanging boulder while Rosie cleaned the fish and impaled them on sticks for roasting.

"Now," Rosie said, "if we just had a couple bottles of champagne, this would be wonderful."

"I'm afraid it's water tonight," Clint said, spreading his bedroll and listening to his empty belly rumble.

When the trout were roasted, they devoured them to the bones, washing the firm white meat down with mountain water and wiping the grease from their lips with the backs of their coat sleeves.

Clint had hobbled the buckskin and the sorrel but let Duke stand free. And now, with a bright canopy of stars overhead, he went to his lame gelding and scratched it behind the ears. Duck nickered his soft appreciation.

"It's been harder on you today than any of us," Clint said, "but if we don't have any trouble tonight or tomorrow, we should be in Prescott by this time tomorrow night. I got a good friend who owns a livery in town. He'll take care of you."

In reply, the horse nuzzled Clint.

"Do you always talk to your horse?" Rosie asked, coming over to join them.

"When we're on the trail I do," Clint said. "He's an exceptionally good listener."

Rosie laughed softly, her face radiant in the starlight. She slipped her arms around Clint's waist and said, "You know what? I'm not so tired anymore."

"We still need sleep."

"I know, but it's very early."

Clint led her over to his bedroll and very soon they were making love under the stars. It wasn't the same hard, passionate lovemaking they'd experienced the night before;

it was slow, but deep and every bit as satisfying.

"Uhhhh!" Rosie moaned when her body began to shudder as Clint exploded inside her.

"Uggh," Clint growled with animal satisfaction.

As soon as he could, Clint pulled up his pants, strapped his holstered gun back on, and warmed his hands over their flickering campfire. With darkness, the night had taken on a chill.

"Aren't you going to sleep now?" Rosie asked.

"In a little while."

"Are you expecting trouble?"

Clint's first thought was to reassure her but then he changed his mind. "Either tonight or tomorrow morning," he said. "That's when I'd come if I were them. I'm going to feed this fire a little higher, then we're going to move our bedrolls about twenty yards higher up in those rocks."

"We are?"

"Yes. If someone is coming, they'll be drawn to our campfire."

Clint pitched more wood on the fire, and he and Rosie moved off a ways, leaving two rolls of horseblankets as decoys.

"Let's go to sleep now," he said when they were settled in for the night, heads resting on their saddles.

The Gunsmith heard an owl hoot somewhere down in the trees and then, way off in the distance, the rumble of thunder. But so far, he heard nothing to cause him any sense of alarm.

"Clint?"

"Do you know what this Ben Towers even looks like?"

"I've never actually seen him," Clint admitted.

A long pause. "But what if he's changed his name? How would we even know the man?"

"Good question. First off, I've heard about him for years. I've had him described to me several times. He's above average height, late thirties and he smokes Mexican cigarillos. I'm told he's also partial to wearing turquoise jewelry. Might have a couple of rings on each hand. Maybe a heavy silver bracelet fashioned by the Hopi or Zuni Indians."

"Is that all? In New Mexico, Colorado and Arizona, a lot of men smoke Mexican cigars and wear fancy turquoise and silver jewelry."

"He'll be packing a Colt on his hip and I can't exactly explain how, but I can tell a real gunman at first glance. They just stand a little different, hands always close to their gun when they're around strangers, eyes moving a lot."

Rosie did not say it, but the Gunsmith also had a way of keeping his right hand near his gun and his eyes were always restless.

"And this salting mines with gold business," Clint added. "It's not an uncommon thing to do, so a man has to be damn good at it to fool people in these times. We'll hear about that too."

"Will he recognize you?"

Clint sighed and pointed out a shooting star to Rosie. "That's a good luck sign," he told her.

"But will he recognize you?" she asked a second time.

"It's possible," Clint admitted.

"I'm not staying in Precott," she told him. "I'm staying with you right to the end."

"There's plenty of time to talk about it later," he said, pulling his hat down over his eyes. "Now let's go to sleep."

"Good night," she whispered, kissing his cheek, and she curled up close at his side.

Clint fell asleep instantly but not soundly. Twice before midnight, the distant roll of thunder awakened him, and once, when Duke stomped the ground with his good forefoot, the Gunsmith sat bolt upright, reaching for his gun.

His campfire was still burning, though low until almost dawn when Duke stomped his hooves and snorted an anxious warning.

Clint was awake in a split second. His hand found the butt of his sixgun, and it came up from under his blankets as fast as the strike of a rattler.

He didn't see them at first. But his gelding did. Duke's ears were pointed in their direction and every muscle in the animal's body was tensed. Clint rolled silently out of his blankets, grabbing his boots and pulling them on when he was behind a rock. He crouched low, aimed his pistol toward the campfire, and waited.

A full minute passed, then another, before Clint saw a shadow emerge from the darkness of the rocks and creep silently toward the decoying saddle blankets. Two more dark silhouettes appeared, and when they were about ten yards from the campfire they froze.

Clint heard one of them whisper. Then he saw them all twist suddenly around, realizing they'd been tricked.

The Gunsmith opened fire. The distance was long and downslope, but he adjusted his aim for that, and the lead man died with a bullet in his brisket. Clint winged the second man, who howled and threw himself into the rocks. The third assassin was smart enough to find cover before he returned fire.

"Clint!"

The Gunsmith pivoted to see a confused and frightened Rosie standing upright. "Get down!"

Rosie turned at the sound of his voice and started toward the Gunsmith but a bullet dropped her to the dirt.

Clint jumped up and raced to her side. With bullets swarming all around him, he pulled the wounded girl behind cover.

Rosie cried, "My leg! I've been shot!"

It was too dark to see anything except the stars dying overhead. "Which leg!" he shouted.

"The right one!"

Clint yanked his bandana from his pocket. When he felt the wet blood on her leg, he fashioned a tourniquet just above the wound.

"It's going to be all right," he told her. "Do you understand me? You've got to stay still and hide until I take care of them."

"All right," she groaned.

"Where's your gun?"

"In my coat."

Clint swore. Her coat was laying beside their bedrolls and he knew better than to go after it.

"Just lie still," he ordered. "I'll be back. I promise."

Rosie gripped his arm with a desperate strength. "How many?" she managed to ask between clenched teeth.

"One dead, one wounded. One wild card yet to play," Clint told her, just as another bullet sprayed them with granite dust.

Clint didn't want to leave Rosie, but he knew that he had little choice. He could not be certain how badly the first man he'd winged was hurt. If his wound was minor, then Clint faced two men instead of just one. Better to go after them than to wait for them to attack.

Staying close to ground and among the rocks, the Gunsmith managed to work his way downhill. Overhead, the sky was just starting to get light, and the visibility improved with each passing moment.

Where the hell did they go! he wondered as he inched forward, poised and ready to fire.

A boot scraped a rock off to his right, and Clint threw himself down on his belly as two bullets whip-cracked through the air he'd just vacated. Clint saw a muzzle-flash and he fired.

A man screamed. Clint thumbed back the hammer of his gun and rolled about three feet to his left, hearing a sound not unlike the flapping of an eagle's wings hard against the sky.

"You sonofabitch!"

Clint twisted around, dropping his hammer and feeling his sixgun buck solidly in his fist. A bullet ate dirt at his side. Clint fired again, and the dark outline of his attacker vanished in the swirling gunsmoke.

The Gunsmith thumbed back his hammer and squirmed across the ground. His heart was thudding against the insides of his ribs, and he was breathing as if he'd been running a foot race.

He waited a full minute before he climbed to his feet and crept around a big boulder to see a man thrashing in death.

Clint knelt by his side. "Who are you?"

A hand fluttered upward toward Clint's throat. He caught it in an iron fist and shook it hard. "Who are you!"

The dying man croaked out a curse. With his free hand, he fumbled to yank free a Bowie knife jammed behind his belt.

Clint stood up and backed off a step. "Mooney sent you, didn't he."

The man's chest was pumping like a bellows. In the strengthening light, he seemed to summon up his last reserves and hissed, "Fuck you!"

"Tough man," Clint said, turning and leaving him to die.

Rosie had taken a bullet in the thigh. It was painful and would hobble her badly for a month or more but now that he had enough light to make a careful examination, Clint could see that the bullet had missed bone and artery.

"We got lucky," Clint said. "You're going to be fine. You just need a doctor as soon as we can find one. Bleeding is almost stopped."

She gripped his hands fiercely. "What about them?"

"They're dead."

"Did they say . . ."

"I couldn't get the last one to talk before he died."

"But it was Mooney, wasn't it?"

"Had to be. But I'd have liked to have had some proof. Not that a dying man's word would have been taken second-hand by any court."

Rosie nodded. "Maybe I won't be able to go with you to Colorado after all."

Clint holstered his gun. "I'm going to fashion a travois and we need to get started just as soon as we can. With you and my lame horse, we sure are going to cause a stir when we drag into Prescott."

"Give them something to gossip about," Rosie said, dredging up a brave smile.

"You bet it will," Clint told her before he loosened the tourniquet a little, made sure that the wound was clotting, and hurried off to break camp and cut a couple of poles.

The poles for their travois were easy enough to fashion, but it took some longer to rig up and stretch saddle blankets between them and get the sorrel mare to consent to pulling the contraption.

It was nearly two hours after sunrise when the Gunsmith was satisfied that the sorrel wouldn't buck or bolt and run away dragging Rosie. He spent another ten minutes relieving the three dead gunmen of weapons, money, and personal belongings of value. But not one of them carried any identification—which, considering their purpose for being here, was not all that surprising.

When he had the sorrel mare all rigged up and Rosie loaded onto the travois, Clint bent down beside her. "I'm damn sorry, but this will be a hard, bumpy ride and pretty slow going. With luck, we'll be in Prescott before midnight."

"I wasn't planning on dancing with the city fellas tonight," she told him.

Clint bent and kissed her lips. "You're a real trooper, Rosie. You're going to make some man a damned fine wife."

"If that's your idea of a marriage proposal, I accept."

"It isn't so you can't accept," the Gunsmith said with a wink before he mounted the buckskin. He slammed his heels into its ribs before it took the notion to start bucking.

Clint reined the gelding toward Prescott, leading the sorrel mare, Duke and poor Rosie stretched out on the crude travois. It was going to be a long, hard day.

SEVEN

Distant lights had pulled Clint and his weary entourage through the last grinding miles until they'd finally stumbled into Prescott long, long after dark. Prescott was an old ranching, timber, and mining community located in a mountain valley surrounded by heavy pine forest and fed by Granite Creek. Over the years, big copper, gold, silver and lead strikes had been discovered in the nearby hills. Clint had spent many a pleasant evening in the saloons that formed a hub around the town square. Now he wasted no time but led the horses and travois directly to Doc Williams's Victorian mansion. The mansion was dark, but when Clint hammered on the front door a light went on upstairs.

"Coming, coming!"

Doc Williams was in his seventies, a conscientious man who had taken up the medical profession in his late thirties after his wife had died in childbirth. Before that, Williams had been a successful Arizona cattle rancher, so going to Harvard Medical School had been quite an adjustment. But Williams had excelled in medical training and returned to become Prescott's most beloved and valued citizen.

"Well, Clint Adams!" the old man snorted, peering through the window before opening his door. "What in the devil brings you here at this hour?"

"There's a young woman resting outside on a travois with a gunshot wound in her leg. Her name is Rosie and we've been traveling since dawn. I'm worried about infection, Doc."

"Well let's get her on in and take a look."

Rosie was dozing and her skin was hot when Clint untied her from the travois and carried her into the house.

"Bring her on in here," the doctor said, leading off down the hallway and turning into a room where he treated after-hours patients. "Lay her on that examination table."

Rosie wakened with a start, her eyes glazed and round with fright. "Clint!"

"It's going to be all right," he promised. "Doc Williams isn't a common tooth puller. He's one of the best. He saved my life a few years back."

"That old bullet wound stiffen up on you yet?" the doctor asked.

Clint shrugged his left shoulder. "Only on cold mornings."

"Give it time," the doctor warned as he turned his full attention to Rosie and began cutting away Rosie's bandages. The Gunsmith held his breath while Doc Williams examined the wound, frowning and gently probing.

"What do you think, Doc?"

"It's a nasty bullet wound and there's already some infection. I'll wash it out real good with solution and treat it with sulfa powders. It's a damn good thing you got here now, instead of tomorrow."

"Could I lose it?" Rosie whispered fearfully.

"I don't think so," the doctor said, turning to wash his hands. "But you're going to have a scar, young lady."

Rosie struggled to sit upright and Clint was forced to hold her down. Only then did he realize that she was a little out of her head with fever and worry. "It'll be all right," he said reassuringly.

"Of course it will," the doctor said. "And right now, I'm going to give you a good strong dose of laudanum for the pain. It'll help you to sleep. When you wake up tomorrow morning, I promise you'll feel much better."

Rosie nodded and took the medicine, swallowing it with a shudder. Clint stayed with them for more than an hour while the doctor cleaned and rebandaged the leg. By then the laudanum had taken its effect and Rosie was out cold.

"She'll sleep until afternoon. I'll have a look at her early tomorrow morning," the doctor said, thumbing Rosie's eyelids up to examine her pupils.

"Is she really going to be all right?"

Doc Williams frowned. "Funny thing about infection, Clint. Sometimes you get it, sometimes you don't. This one has already set in and it's going to be a fight. My guess is that we'll save her leg. What happened?"

Clint told the doctor about being attacked at dawn in the mountains north of Prescott.

"Any idea who or why?"

"I've got ideas, but no proof." Clint frowned. "Can I leave her in your care for a few weeks?"

"Why sure! My crotchety old housekeeper and her husband sleep upstairs but there are still three empty bedrooms. We can take care of her just fine."

"I'll make sure you're well paid for your trouble," Clint promised. "I'd make arrangements myself except that I've got to get over to Colorado on business."

The doctor was wise enough not to ask Clint what kind of business was so urgent that he would leave a frightened and wounded girl behind. "Whenever you get back, she'll be here. Pretty little thing, isn't she."

"She sure is."

"She uh . . . kind of special to you?"

"Yeah." Clint frowned. "If you have something to say, spit it out."

"Well," the doctor said, "it's just that there are some fine young bachelors in Prescott who are going to be mighty interested in a girl as pretty as this one—even with a bullet in her thigh."

"I'm not planning on marrying her," Clint said. "And as for your 'fine young bachelors,' well, bring them on. Rosie is the kind of girl who can make up her own mind about such things. She sure doesn't need my permission to see other men."

"You want to tell me anything about her background?"

"Nope." Clint put his hand on the doctor's thin shoulder. "Her past life is past. She's made mistakes, but haven't we all? Let's just say she's starting over fresh."

The doctor arched his brow. "With a bullet wound."

"Yes," Clint said, "with a bullet wound."

The doctor shrugged. "All right. It's fine with me. I just know people are going to ask."

"Let them ask her. Rosie will tell them whatever she wants."

"Fair enough."

Clint left a few minutes later. He mounted the buckskin who was too exhausted to buck, then led the sorrel mare, the empty travois, and Duke up through the dark deserted back streets of town until he reached a stable on the southern edge of Prescott. A lantern burned through a dirty window in the barn, and Clint heaved a big sigh when his call brought a short, powerful man hobbling out in his nightshirt.

"Eli, it's me. Clint Adams."

"Well I'll be damned!" Eli exclaimed, lowering a big Army Colt. "Step down offa that ugly buckskin and come inside. Say, what the hell is that thing you got dragging along behind that poor sorrel? And how come you ain't riding Duke?"

"It's a long story," Clint said. "Duke is lame and I'm going to need to leave him with you for awhile, Eli. I can't think of anyone else I'd trust."

Eli scratched his slightly protruding belly. He was a bull of a man with great thick arms, almost no neck and a bald head. Once he'd been a bare knuckle fighter and had earned a pile of money along with a face full of scars, a squished nose and smashed knuckles. With his fight earnings, he'd bought this livery and had prospered. It was said that he was the most even-tempered man in Arizona until he saw someone mistreating an animal.

Clint led Duke and the other horses into the barn. After Eli had inspected the hoof and prescribed his own form of treatment, Clint told his friend to grain the buckskin and have the animal ready to ride tomorrow.

"But you only just got here!" Eli protested.

"Got to leave," Clint said, his face grim and set from fatigue and the strain of worrying about Rosie. "Like I said, I've got important business in Colorado."

"Gun business I'll bet."

When Clint didn't respond, Eli said, "Hey, want to sleep here? I've an extra cot in the tack room. Won't cost you anything and I'll buy you breakfast."

"I'm planning to sleep through breakfast. Make it lunch."

"You're on," Eli said. "Now let's get these horses fed and watered so we can go to sleep."

That was just fine with the Gunsmith. It had been one hell of a long day, and the immediate future did not look to be much easier.

Clint and Eli grained all three horses liberally before retiring, and when the Gunsmith finally eased his weary bones down on the cot and closed his eyes he was asleep in minutes. He did not awaken until eleven o'clock the next morning, and would have slept even longer if Eli hadn't given his cot a hard shove.

"Let's go get something to eat," the liveryman said. "I've been working since daylight and my guts are growlin'."

Clint pushed himself to his feet and rubbed the sleep from his eyes. "Did you get a better look at Duke's hoof this morning?"

"I did. I'm going to soak it with Epsom salts, then pack the hoof with cotton and grease. That's the best thing in the world for a rock bruise. I'm also worried that Duke might have injured a tendon limping all the way over from Quartz.

Doc Wright's Horse Liniment is the best thing I ever seen for a stretched tendon or pulled muscles. I even use it on myself."

Clint remembered the liveryman in Quartz had said Doc Wright's Liniment was worthless, which only proved that one man's medicine was another's poison.

"Let's go eat," the Gunsmith said, "I'm hungry too."

They had a good steak and fried potatoes and then Clint hurried over to see Rosie. She was awake and her color was much improved.

"You look a lot better today," Clint told her.

"I feel better. Dr. Williams is a wonderful man. He's asked me to stay right here in this beautiful house until I feel up to moving."

"I'm going to be leaving for Colorado in a little while," Clint said.

Rosie's eyes widened with sudden concern so Clint quickly added, "But I'll return just as soon as I've found Miss Mullane's daughter."

"But what if . . ."

"Rosie," he said patiently, "there's a telegraph office here and I promise to keep you informed. In the meantime, I want you to rest and enjoy yourself. After I return with Lisa, we can talk about the future. Until then, I think you ought to get acquainted with some of the people in this town. Especially the bachelors."

"Clint, you're the only man that interests me."

"I'm not the marrying kind," he said looking her right in the eye. "What you need is a man who wants to raise a family. A settled man."

"I'll take you settled or not."

Clint shook his head. He was flattered, but a little concerned. "Just promise me you'll be nice to any callers, Rosie. Smile at them, act like the lady I know you are."

"You sound like a mother talking."

Clint blushed. "I just want what's best for you. In Prescott, you've got a chance for something better than you've ever had before."

"I wanted to go with you," she said. "But since I can't, just come back safe with that little girl."

"I will," Clint promised. "With any luck, I'll return by the time you're all healed and ready to ride."

"What happened to my mare?"

"She's over at my friend Eli's stable. As soon as you're able, check on her and Duke. Maybe bring them a little sugar."

"I will." Rosie gave Clint a big, wet kiss. "I'll be thinking about you every minute of every day."

Clint turned to leave, feeling good that Rosie was looking so much better. It was also satisfying to know that she would be safe here in a nice house with good people all around to care for her.

"Wait!" she called just as he was going out the door.

Clint turned. "What for?"

Rosie rummaged through her baggage and pulled out a handful of money. "Here. You've got enough to worry about without adding money to it."

Clint hesitated. "No more than a hundred dollars, and it's just a loan."

"You saved my life, so please don't be so stubborn."

The Gunsmith took the money, knowing he'd pay her back when his luck finally changed. Right now, he needed to buy supplies and ammunition. And once he reached Colorado, it helped if a man could spread a little money around when asking folks questions.

"This morning I asked Doc Williams if he'd ever heard of Ben Towers."

"And he said?"

"He told me that Ben Towers gunned down two men at the plaza and one of his stray bullets hit a little boy in the arm. Ben Towers didn't give a damn. He went to a saloon and played cards as if nothing had ever happened. Doc called Ben Towers a cold-blooded killer."

"So I've heard."

"If you find him, shoot first, Clint! Don't take any chances."

"I won't," Clint promised as he tipped his hat in farewell and headed out the door.

EIGHT

It felt strange taking off for Colorado on the buckskin gelding instead of Duke. When a man was riding a long trail, he wanted a horse that he could trust. This one was about half outlaw, to Clint's way of thinking. Not that it had done anything wrong except wanting to buck whenever he swung into the saddle. The buckskin had not tried to kick or bite or run away, but it still acted quirky enough that the Gunsmith didn't trust it.

"I'm going to name you Squirrel," he told the buckskin that night when he made camp and the animal pulled back when he tried to put hobbles on its forelegs.

The buckskin snorted and rolled its eyes warily. Clint shook his head with disgust. He'd picked a real screwball, though the horse was obviously strong and had plenty of speed and endurance.

He slept well that night even though he did not have the comfort of knowing that his horse would alert him in case of danger. In the morning, however, Clint was astonished to see that the buckskin had disappeared.

"You sonofabitch!" he swore, grabbing his bridle and heading off to find the animal.

It was easy to see the buckskin's tracks, and Clint was a good enough tracker to read how the buckskin had hopped away despite the hobbles. A lot of horses could do that, but they'd soon tire unless they were mighty determined to put some ground between themselves and their owners.

Clint was furious. He went back and broke camp, threw his saddle over his shoulder, and carried his bedroll and rifle.

Two hard hours of tracking brought him up to the edge of a mountain meadow where he saw the buckskin tied in front of a cabin. A large bearded man wearing a fringed buckskin shirt was brushing the horse. In a nearby corral, a big mule was pacing restlessly back and forth.

The Gunsmith frowned. It was his experience that mountain men were not very sociable and considered themselves to be a law unto themselves. In the case of his horse, Clint could foresee a problem in the making.

"Hello there!" Clint shouted in greeting.

The mountain man jerked around quick, dropped the brush and disappeared inside his cabin. A moment later, Clint saw the barrel of a .50-caliber hunting rifle poke out of the cabin like a finger of death. The Gunsmith threw himself down just as the rifle belched fire and smoke.

"Hey!" Clint shouted, lifting his head. "What the hell is the matter with you! That's my buckskin horse I come for!"

"You can have him over my dead body!"

Clint swore in anger. What kind of a fool was he dealing with, anyway?

"I hobbled him last night and he run off."

"The hell with that, he's mine!"

"Listen you fool, we can backtrack to my camp and that'll prove he ran away from me!"

In reply, the mountain man jumped out and fired another round. The bullet cut a path of dead meadow grass all the way to the crown of the Gunsmith's Stetson. The hat went sailing and Clint shouted in fury.

"That's it, you idiot!" he cried, jumping up and racing toward the cabin. He knew the mountain man was firing a single-shot black-powder rifle.

The mountain man must have felt Clint coming at him. He poked his head out the door, saw Clint running forward at full speed, and knew he was not going to have time to reload.

The man swapped ends of his hunting rifle and came charging out of the door swinging the rifle like a club.

Clint ducked, feeling the air move overhead and hearing the wind whistle. He could have drawn his pistol and opened a hole in the mountain man's gut. Instead, he punched low.

"Ahhhh!" the big man cried, dropping the rifle and cupping his crotch.

The Gunsmith stepped back and resisted the temptation of hitting the man in his gaping mouth. Instead, he picked up the big black-powder rifle and waited a moment for the mountain man to quit howling.

That took several minutes. When anger began to replace pain in the big man's eyes, Clint drew his gun and said, "If you come at me again, I'll shoot off what I didn't crush with my fist."

That brought the mountain man up short. He was still clutching at his crotch and in a great deal of pain.

"You didn't have to do that!" he choked.

"Sure I did or you'd have brained me with that rifle. Besides, I told you that all I wanted was my horse back."

"But I found him runnin' free!"

"No you didn't. You found him hopping along in your meadow and you caught him, then cut away his hobbles."

The mountain man glared at him. "What a man can catch, he deserves to keep."

"Oh yeah? Well, that kind of thinking has gotten a lot of men hanged as horse thieves," Clint said. "Now I'm going to take this horse back, and if you try and grab up that rifle I'll blow a hole in your arm and you'll really have something to howl about. Is that understood?"

"Damn you! I need a horse!"

"Well, I ain't carrying a saddle around for the exercise," Clint barked.

"You want to sell that horse?"

"No."

"What about a trade?" The mountain man jerked his thumb toward his corral. "That's the finest mule in the whole damned Arizona Territory. He'll outwalk or outrun any horse—including that buckskin."

"If he's so good, why would you trade him?"

" 'Cause he hates my guts," the man grunted. "I tied him to a tree and beat the piss outa him about a week ago, and ever since, he's had blood in his eye for me."

Clint frowned. He really didn't want a mule to ride, especially a big man-hater like this one appeared to be. On the other hand, he wasn't overly fond of the buckskin. The horse bucked, shied and could not be hobbled. Most likely, he'd even chew through a good rope.

"How do I know that mule wouldn't hate me too?"

The mountain man managed to dredge up a malicious smile. "There's only one way to find out, ain't there?"

Clint frowned. He knew that a good mule was prized by most men because they were steadier and more sure-footed than a horse. And because Clint was going into the Colorado high mountain country, it would not be a bad idea to have a very sure-footed animal.

"Ah," he said, "I don't know. That mule of yours looks pretty ornery to me."

"Why, he ain't! I paid . . . paid a hundred dollars cash money for him."

"Oh bullshit."

"Well I did! Just come on over here and take a look at him. You'll see he's a young'n and damn near as tall as your horse. He's a damn sight smarter, too."

"Yeah," Clint said, "I know a little bit about mules. They are smart enough to get a man if they're vicious."

"But this one ain't! He just hates me is all. Why, if you was to sweet-talk him a little. Maybe give him something out of your saddlebags, he'd be your friend for life."

Clint glanced over at the buckskin, which rolled its eyes crazily and snorted. "All right," he said. "Let's take a look at the mule."

The mountain man grinned. "You're gonna like him if you can get close enough to pet him. That much old Abe will guarantee."

Clint made sure that he did not let "old Abe" get behind him as they walked over to the corral to study the mule.

As soon as Abe was at the fence, however, the mule flattened its long ears and lunged at the man, its head and yellow teeth snaking between the poles and damn near getting ahold of the mountain man.

"You crazy yellow-toothed bastard!" Abe cursed. "I should have shoved that limb up your ass the other day."

Clint studied the big mule and then he shook his head and turned away. "To hell with that," he said. "I've got problems enough without letting a man-killer like him into my life. You keep your mule, Abe. I want no part of him."

The mountain man protested bitterly but Clint paid him no mind. He went back and untied his horse, then led it out to the meadow where he'd been fired upon and had dropped his saddle, bedroll and rifle. In ten minutes, he was ready to go.

"Now behave yourself," Clint said to the buckskin before he jammed his boot into the stirrup. "If you try and buck me off this time, I might just shove my Winchester up your ass and pull the trigger."

But the buckskin either didn't understand or didn't believe him. At any rate, Clint's right leg was still swinging over his saddle when the big horse took the bit into his mouth, ducked his hammer head and started to buck. The Gunsmith tried desperately to get his right boot jammed through his stirrup, but he never had a chance. Three mighty bucks sent Clint skyward, and he did a complete flip before he crashed to the grass with the air slamming out of his lungs.

Clint sucked for air, and just when he thought he had it he looked up to see the mountain man standing over him with that big rifle of his raised overhead.

"Mister," Abe said, "I ought to brain you for punchin' me in the balls. I ought to split your head open like a gourd—

but I ain't going to do it if you will agree to make the trade—with you throwing in your saddle and bridle."

Clint knew he had no choice but to agree. Besides, he was ready to shoot the buckskin, which was getting crazier every day.

"All right," he wheezed. "It's a deal."

"You mean it?" Abe's bearded face reflected shock.

"I do."

Abe lowered his rifle. "Then go collect my mule and git!"

Clint managed to struggle to his feet. Abe retreated a step, the rifle still raised overhead. Clint could have drawn his sixgun and shot the man before he could react, but all he wanted to do was leave this place far behind.

The Gunsmith bent and grabbed his bedroll, saddlebags and a gunnysack of provisions. "I won't say it's been good to know you," he growled. "But so long. You deserve whatever comes to you from that horse of mine."

"Oh, I'll make a gentleman outa him, all right," the mountain man vowed. "You can beat a horse into behavin', but not a big mule!"

"Well you can just keep them both," Clint said, starting off on foot toward Colorado and wondering if his luck was ever going to change.

"Well, you're taking him!"

Clint didn't look back. He just shook his head and kept walking.

"Come on, Mister!" Abe's voice was pleading. "We had a deal!"

Clint was half way across the meadow when he heard the mountain man whoop. Clint turned to see the mule going after Abe, who just did make it inside his cabin to slam his door.

For the first time in days, Clint grinned. "That big sonofabich sure does hate him," he said to himself.

The mule began to bray so loud that the sound of it echoed into the hills and then back again. After a few minutes, the mule spotted Clint, and damned if it didn't come after him!

The Gunsmith wasn't about to run. He was still feeling the effects of having the wind knocked out of his lungs. He dropped his bedroll, drew his Winchester out of its scabbard, and stood his ground.

"Let's just see how smart you really are," he growled, taking aim on the animal's chest.

The mule, it turned out, was plenty smart. Smart enough to know what a rifle could do to man or animal. It skidded to a halt, stared at Clint and then brayed mournfully.

The Gunsmith lowered his rifle, but he kept it ready as he hoisted his bedroll and gunnysack of supplies.

"I tell you," Clint said before he started off again. "When a man's luck turns bad, everything he touches goes sour."

The mule watched him trudge along for several minutes. It turned its head to study the cabin, then started after the Gunsmith.

By sundown, Clint was footsore and damn tired of walking. The mule had followed him like a pet dog the whole day. As Clint made his camp, the animal began to graze nearby.

"I hope a grizzly bear comes to eat you," Clint said as he munched on an apple and started his fire.

The mule raised its head, brayed in answer, and watched him. Clint threw the beast what remained of his apple, and the mule trotted right up and ate it.

"I ought to shoot you now so I don't have to worry that you're going to come after me when I fall asleep. Be just like a smart mule to do that."

The mule's nostrils twitched and Clint knew its mind was on another apple. "Here," he said, digging into his gunnysack before tossing the mule another apple.

The big animal ate with surprising delicacy. It moved in close to the campfire. After Clint had eaten and his eyelids began to droop, the mule yawned, showing its huge yellow teeth, lay down, and promptly fell asleep.

The Gunsmith allowed himself to smile. One thing about mules, they had a lot of personality. Most of them acted more like huge, overgrown dogs than cousins to the horse.

Clint kept his sixgun and rifle handy, but he had a hunch that he wouldn't need them to kill the mule. The animal probably had been a good one once, before the mountain man tried to beat it into submission.

Clint stretched out and studied the heavens above. It would have been very easy to feel sorry for himself. Now he had no horse and the San Juan Mountains lay just ahead. It was hard not to admit that he was in a poor situation. But at least he had that money Rosie had given him to buy a good horse when he came to the next town. The buckskin had been good physically, but not mentally. Kind of like this big, handsome mule with the sweet, apple-scented breath.

NINE

The next morning Clint was rudely awakened by the sound of loud braying in his ears. He grabbed his pistol, and, still asleep, cocked back to the hammer into the face of the big mule—a face covered with flour.

"Damn you!" Clint shouted, twisting around to see that the mule had looted his gunnysack and devoured not only his flour, but also the rest of the apples.

In reply, the mule brayed again then stared at him with big, curious eyes. Clint wanted to pull the trigger of his Colt, but the mule looked so lonesome and curious that he could not do it.

"All right," Clint stormed. "You've eaten half my supplies, now you're going to have to earn them!"

The Gunsmith holstered his gun and broke camp without any breakfast. He fashioned a rope halter, then gathered his remaining supplies. He shoved his rifle into his bedroll and slung the whole thing over his shoulder.

"You're either carrying me into Colorado or I'm going to find out what the Apache think is so special about roasted mule meat."

The mule flicked its long rabbit ears back and forth and looked so innocent that Clint fashioned a pair of reins and hopped onto his back, balancing his belongings. To his great surprise, the mule did not move until he reined it toward Colorado and clucked his tongue. Then, the mule headed northeast like he'd smelled a bucket of oats and molasses.

It was a good day and they made twenty-five miles at least. They would have made even more if the Gunsmith had been able to stand the pounding. Unfortunately, he had no saddle. Fortunately, the mule's back was broad and its gait was easy.

At noon, Clint had reined in the mule and taken a short nap while the animal had grazed nearby. Waking refreshed, he'd fashioned his bedroll into a riding pad, and the afternoon had been much more pleasant.

"I don't know exactly where we're heading," he told the mule that night, "but wherever it is, you're going a long ways toward getting us there."

The mule brayed, and its eyes looked sorrowful as it studied Clint's gunnysack.

"Sorry, no more apples or flour. I'm afraid you're out of luck tonight."

Two days later, Clint was climbing the high and ruggedly beautiful plateau country that led him into southwestern Colorado. This was red-rock country, wild with mostly juniper and *piñon* pine. Higher up, he would move into the conifer and fir tree country where there were still grizzly roaming in almost unexplored canyons and over tall mountains capped year round by snow.

The mule was a remarkable animal. On the steepest, narrowest trails, it moved like a cat walking a fencetop. It watched its rather dainty feet and could place all four of them in a straight line whenever necessary. Clint had never spent much time on a mule, but he quickly became convinced that this one was far safer to ride on the winding little mountain game trails than the best of horses, his own Duke included.

Five days of hard riding brought them into a rugged little mining town called Hard Times. The town seemed aptly named because its gold was petering out and already there were a number of shops boarded up and closed for business.

But once, Hard Times must have been good times, because the main street was at least two hundred yards long and Clint even passed a church and a schoolhouse.

He was aware that he made a strange and a curious sight riding into town. School was in recess. When a number of the children saw him come trotting in on his mule, they rushed to their schoolyard's picket fence to giggle and point. Clint didn't mind. He tipped his bullet-riddled hat and grinned.

"Can you tell me if this town still has a sheriff?"

"Sure, Mister! His name is Sheriff Vickery and his office is right next to the barber shop. You can't miss it!"

"Thank you," Clint said, continuing on to the sheriff's office.

He slipped off the mule, feeling a dull ache in his crotch and vowing to find a saddle before he continued on. Clint started to tie the mule but, to his surprise and anger, the beast pulled back and began to bray. A nearby saddle horse, unfamiliar with a riding mule, spooked and also reared back, breaking his reins and galloping down the street.

"Hey!" a man yelled angrily. "That was my horse!"

"Well then, what are you doing standing here jawing at me for?" Clint demanded. "Go after the damned spooky thing!"

The man was packing a gun and he looked furious but when Clint's own hand shaded his Colt some kind of understanding passed between them and the man abruptly took off after his horse.

"What's the matter with you?" Clint asked the mule, trying to calm it down and tie it up. But the mule wouldn't tie. The minute Clint started to wrap his crude rope reins around the hitching rail, the beast yanked back, snorting and braying. All up and down the main street, horses were beginning to snort with fear.

"You'd best leave him just stand there," an old man said.

"Who the hell are you?"

"Just an old mule skinner who understands them fine critters better than you ever will," the man said. "And it don't take a lot of brains to see that your mule won't tolerate being tied up. So just let him be."

"Well what if he walks away?"

"Then you find him somewhere nearby," the man said. "But I'll tell you this. Even if you could get him tied, he'd just pull that hitch rail out of the ground and then the sheriff would arrest you and make you pay for another."

Clint had a feeling this old man knew what he was talking about. "All right," he sighed. "But if he goes wandering off and gets hurt or in trouble, I won't claim him."

"He won't 'get hurt,' " the old man said. "Why, he'll lick any horse on this street. Besides, I'll watch him for two bits an hour."

"You got a deal," Clint said. "Will you also watch my bedroll?"

"Why sure, for another dime."

Clint ground his teeth in anger. "Maybe, since you know mules so well, you'd like to buy this one."

"Got no money. But if I did, I'd give you fifty dollars for him."

"Well, I'd take it," Clint said. "What's your sheriff's name?"

"Matt Vickery."

"He any good?"

"Nope."

"I need to talk to him anyway," Clint said, going inside.

Matt Vickery was heavyset and sloppy. His office was cluttered, there were globs of wet tobacco juice on his floor where he hadn't bothered to use his own spitoon and it was obvious from the mussed bed and dirty dishes on a crude wooden table that his office was also his home. That wasn't rare in a small town where the citizens paid so little a wage that the law could not afford to even rent a hotel room. What was rare was the complete lack of pride or professionalism that Clint saw in both the man and his surroundings.

"You the sheriff?"

"That's right."

"Then you should wear your badge," Clint bluntly told the man.

Vickery's jaw pushed out aggressively. He pulled his pants up closer to his belly button and leaned forward. "Mister, I don't like people telling me how to act or do my job. So you just keep your opinions to your own self. Hear now?"

"I'm looking for a man named Ben Towers," Clint said, coming right to the point. "Maybe you've heard of him?"

"Sure!" Vickery chuckled but it wasn't a nice sound. "But you're a lookin' for a ghost. Ben Towers was gunned down trying to break out of the Arizona Territory Prison down in Yuma."

"Uh-uh," Clint said. "He escaped. Probably changed his appearance. Maybe grew a a full beard. Maybe even colored his hair a little. Don't matter. He's free and he's in Colorado salting mines and creating his usual mischief."

Vickery studied him closely. "What are you, a U.S. Marshal or a bounty hunter?"

"Neither."

"Then what?"

Without giving any names, Clint told him about Lucy Mullane's daughter and why he wanted to find Towers. "He's a bad one and he hasn't gotten religion," Clint ended. "The sooner I find him, the sooner I rid Colorado of a tough customer and bring a little girl back to her real mother."

Vickery rubbed his chin. "If what you say is true, there's got to be a reward out on him somewhere. Come on, how much is it?"

"I told you—no reward."

"I think you're either lying or you're crazy."

Clint advanced a step. He was seething as he poked his finger at the man. "Listen, you've got to be the sorriest excuse I ever saw for a sheriff. That's this town's problem, though. All I want to know is if you've ever seen or heard

of anyone salting mines around here and if they fit Ben
Towers's general description."

Vickery swallowed. "Sure mines have been salted in these
parts. Every time we hear of a new strike, the first thing you
think about is that it has probably been salted and someone
is trying to sell off shares to the suckers for their cash. But
I never heard of Ben Towers being in these parts."

"The girl I'm looking for is about six."

"You got a picture of her?"

"No."

"Well then how are you supposed to recognize her even
if you find her?"

Clint didn't have a good answer to that one. Before he'd
left, Lucy Mullane had given him a general description of
her daughter but it was one that would fit plenty of six-
year-olds. Blue eyes. Blond hair. Pretty. It was a worthless
description, really.

"Well?" Vickery prodded. "How you gonna do it?"

"I can't recognize her," Clint said. "Ben Towers has to
do it."

"And he's going to do that out of the goodness of his
heart?" the sheriff asked sarcastically.

"Go to hell," Clint said, turning for the door.

"Wait!"

Clint's hand was on the doorknob when he turned.
"Yeah?"

"You look like trouble to me," Vickery said. "I want you
out of Hard Times by tomorrow noon."

"And if I don't?"

"You'll be arrested. Jailed. Fined and run out at gun-
point."

Clint smiled. "It'd almost be worthwhile staying just to
see the look on your face when you stare down my gun
barrel, Sheriff."

The Gunsmith returned outside to see the old man feeding
the mule a handful of dried raisins. The mule looked as
gentle and happy as a puppy dog. It was hard to believe he

was the same animal that had tried to bite Abe the mountain man's head off a week before.

"What you gonna do now?" the old man asked.

"Find a livery and see if he'd stand to be penned up and grained for the night," Clint said, taking his reins. "Then tomorrow morning, I'll ride on."

"Fine mule. I'd give you sixty dollars if I had it. Yes sir! I do like this mule."

"And I can see that he likes you and those raisins."

The old man winked. "You keep a pocketful of 'em and you can make a mule into a pussycat. Make him do damn near anything you want for them raisins."

Clint chuckled. "You got any more or do I have to go to a general store for 'em."

"I'll go for you."

"How much?"

"Four bits plus the price of the raisins."

"All right." Clint dug three dollars out of his pocket. "And buy me some flour and apples if they got any."

The man nodded happily. "Only stable in town is just two blocks farther up the street. I'll bring the raisins and flour along. Don't worry."

Clint nodded and the old man hurried away. The Gunsmith shook his head and said to the mule, "I've probably just given away good money."

But an hour later when the mule was in a stall contentedly eating hay and nibbling grain, the old man appeared and not only did he have a bag of raisins and a sack of flour, but also change.

"Keep it," the Gunsmith said. "And by the way, have you ever heard of a man named Ben Towers?"

"Sure! He was gunned down trying to escape from Yuma Prison. Everybody knows that! Why'd ya ask?"

"Ah, never mind," Clint said with a shake of his head.

Finding Ben Towers was going to prove even harder than finding a needle in a haystack—it was going to be like snatching a handful of ghost.

TEN

As long as Clint had a pocketful of raisins, he never had a lick of trouble from the big mule, whom he'd taken to calling Rusty because of the redness in his dark coat. Clint bought a good, used saddle, and everything would have been fine during the next few weeks of traveling about the southwestern corner of Colorado if only he'd have gotten a lead or two on the whereabouts of Ben Towers. But in one town after another he was told that Ben Towers had died in a prison breakout at Yuma.

It wasn't until Clint reached the flourishing mining town of Madrid that he finally got his first lead. He'd gone directly to the sheriff's office, as he always did, more often than not to be viewed suspiciously and even warned to get out of town if he had no honest business. But Madrid's old sheriff recognized him right away.

"Why Clint Adams! Damned if I ain't honored to finally have a chance to see you after ten years."

The man pumped Clint's hand hard as he explained. "I saw you down in El Paso ten years ago and you were helping Sheriff Kidd stand up against an outlaw band that was using both sides of the border. I remember that you finally got so exasperated at the sheriff that you rode across the border into Juarez and shot it out with the outlaws."

"It was either that or walk away and see them mock justice."

"How many men did you kill in Old Mexico that day?"

"Enough," Clint said.

"Some said four, others six and even eight."

"Wrong on all counts," Clint said. "I had to kill three. Just three. The others headed deep into Mexico. I was in no condition to ride after them, so they escaped with their lives."

The sheriff shook his head with admiration. "I was standing in that crowd at the Rio Grande River when you came riding back across and I thought you stood twenty feet tall. I was a stagecoach driver then. Seeing what you did made me decide to try my hand at becoming the law."

"I hope you don't hold that against me," Clint said with a half-smile.

"Oh, hell no! I admit that I was a little long in the tooth to go into this line of work. I had to talk a blue streak to get my first job as a deputy. But it worked out. I was deputy in three towns before I finally rode up this way. The sheriff before me got shot up real bad trying to break up a fight in the local whorehouse. He retired and I offered to take his place."

"It's a nice town," Clint said.

"It'll do. We have some good folks here but we're losing some of 'em as the mines play out. In fact, things have gotten so bad around here that the city council had a meeting last week and figured that they couldn't afford to pay me anymore."

"I'm sorry to hear that."

"Yeah," the sheriff said. "I'll be out of a job tomorrow as a matter of fact. Of course, if I agreed to stay on without wages, that would make the town mighty happy."

"A man has got to eat," Clint said.

"Well, that's what I told them. But they insisted the money isn't in the budget for my pay. They had to spend it all this summer helping the families of a mine cave-in we suffered. It was terrible thing. I don't begrudge what they did, but I'm a little old to be out hunting another job."

For the next twenty minutes, the Gunsmith listened sympathetically as the paunchy, gray-haired sheriff, whose name was Andy Lane, expressed his worries about the future of Madrid and his own welfare. Clint formed a picture of a nice, genial man who'd been lucky enough to stay alive in a business he probably wasn't very well suited for.

"I've never had to shoot a man," Lane bragged. "Oh, I've pistol-whipped a few. But mostly, it's my experience that if you just talk reasonable to a man, he'll listen. You treat people with respect, they'll treat you the same. I think the days of a sheriff being heavy-handed with a sixgun are over."

"You may be right," Clint said, not believing a word of it. "But there are plenty of men who are just plain bad to the bone. They'll shoot you in the guts just to watch you suffer and die. I think a sheriff has to give himself the benefit of the doubt and protect his life. He can't be much good to his community if he's killed because he was too trusting."

Lane filled a smoking pipe and used two matches getting it going. "Well, I would never argue with a legend like you are, Gunsmith. But all the same, I seen and heard of too many lawman that were nothing but legal killers themselves."

Clint was wearying of this conversation. Andy Lane was a very decent man. During the years Clint had been a sheriff and a federal marshal, he'd hired a few nice fellas like Andy and almost always, they either got hurt or killed.

"I'm looking for a man," Clint said, wanting to get to the point of his visit. "I'm sure you've heard of him—his real name is Ben Towers."

"Ben Towers? Why sure I have! But say, he died down in Yuma. You see, there was this prison . . ."

"No," Clint interrupted. "Ben actually escaped and I have reason to believe he's salting mines in this Colorado Territory."

"Salting mines?"

"Among other things, I'd suspect. But I wanted to ask if you've had any of that business here in Madrid in the last year or so."

The sheriff frowned, puffed a little faster on his pipe. "As a matter of fact, we did have quite a case of salting here about six months ago."

"Did you catch whoever was behind it?"

"No," Lane sighed, "and the people who lost their money on the deal have never forgiven me. It was called the . . . my God!"

"What!"

"The mine that was salted was called the Tower Mine. It was over by on the west fork of the creek that runs through Madrid. Big mine that had been closed for about six years. All of a sudden, there were rumors that the new owners were shipping gold out of her. You know how that kind of rumor will build and build."

"I know. But did anyone actually see the gold?"

"Well hell yes!" Lane exclaimed. "Being as how I was sheriff and not wanting to see anyone cheated when there was talk of the mine selling public shares, I went to the assay office and then to our banker. Both men assured me that, yes, not only was the gold high grade, it was being very profitably mined."

"But it wasn't."

"No." Sheriff Lane expelled a deep sigh of regret. "As it turned out, the assayer and the banker were in cahoots with the people at the Tower Mine. They sold shares totaling almost a half million dollars."

"And no one even inspected the mine!"

"Sure we did!" Lane said angrily. "Why I even had a look at it myself. I saw the gold veins in the rock walls. We had some veteran miners and they saw it too. I'll never forget that day. Madrid went wild. Everyone celebrated. It looked like the Tower Mine was going to keep this town on the map right up into the next century."

"So what happened?" Clint asked, figuring he could just about fill in the rest of the story.

"Well, for a few months, everything went along just fine. The Tower Mining Company stock just kept rising and rising. More and more gold was coming out but not nearly as much as the stock prices warranted. Finally, one day the stock began to fall. A day later, the mine was closed and the mine owner was gone."

"What about the assayer and the banker?"

"Gone too," Sheriff Lane muttered. "It took about another day for us to figure out we'd been swindled and swindled big time. Of course, I formed a posse. We hunted high and wide for them three crooked sonsabitches. But they were long gone."

Clint stood up and began to pace back and forth. "Describe the three of them to me."

"Well the assayer was about my age. Short, but bald as a billiard. Nice fella. Wore spectacles and seemed real honest."

"What about the banker?"

"My age again. But tall and dignified. He'd opened his bank about a year before. Seemed real professional. Gave generously to the town charities. Was a member of the Presbyterian Church and the volunteer fire department. Hell of a nice fella."

"All right. What about the owner of the mine?"

"He was about your height. Six foot?"

"A little over," Clint said.

"All right. Slender. About your age, too. His hair was black as an Indian's. Had gray eyes that could look right through you but was real quiet and nice. Said he had been trained as a mining engineer."

"Did he by any chance wear jewelry?"

The sheriff nodded. "It was his vanity, I suppose. He liked silver and turquoise jewelry. Had some beautiful pieces that must have cost him plenty—even buying directly from the Indians."

"That's him," Clint said, banging the sheriff's desk with excitement. "That was Ben Towers."

"Are you sure? He talked once before the town council. Said he and his mining company were here to stay. Talked about how many men he'd come to employ and how it would benefit Madrid. Why, after that talk, a lot of folks wanted him to run for mayor."

"That was Ben Towers," Clint said with certainty. "He's apparently as smooth with his tongue as he is with a gun. And I'll bet you never saw him unless he was wearing a sidearm."

"Oh, he carried one all the time. But of course, I just figure that, having money, it was the prudent thing to do."

"He ever get into a gunfight here in Madrid?"

"Not exactly."

Clint frowned. "What does that mean?"

"Well," Lane hedged. "He did shoot a couple of fellas that tried to rob him. But he came right to my office and sat down and wrote out a full report."

"Any witnesses?"

"No, but . . ."

Clint smiled grimly. "The man is a professional killer, not a mining engineer. And as much as I want to find him, I'm really looking for his daughter."

"Well she was here last winter for while."

"She was!"

"Sure. Cute as a bug. Little girl about six or seven. Blond hair. Blue eyes. Gonna be a beauty some day."

This piece of news stunned Clint and it must have shown by his expression because the sheriff said, "What's wrong?"

"She was supposed to be living with another woman. Maybe foster parents. I don't know for sure. Where did she go?"

"Beats me. But Mr. Slade—that's what he called himself—he told everyone that the climate was too hard on his daughter's health so he sent her down to Arizona where it was warm and dry."

"Did he say exactly where?"

"No, he did not."

Clint expelled a sigh of disappointment. For a moment, he thought that he might have had little Lisa within his grasp. Now, he was back to the square one where he'd started. It all came down to finding Ben Towers first. He was the key to locating the little girl.

"So this Slade fella was really Ben Towers?"

"That's right," Clint said. "And he was in cahoots with the banker and the assayer. I'm pretty sure that, when I find one of them, I'll find all three. Most likely, they've relocated to some other unsuspecting mining town and are putting their swindle into motion right now. Opening the assay office, the new bank and finding an old, abandoned mine to salt with gold."

Sheriff Lane sucked wetly on his pipe. "Why those tricky sonsabitches! They even got a thousand dollars of my own money!"

"I'll try to recover what I can," Clint said. "But my guess is that it'll be all spent. Starting a bank, assay office and a mine—not to mention all the gold they need to salt it so that even experienced miners wouldn't suspect the game— must cost thousands and thousands of dollars."

"They broke the heart of my town," the sheriff said bitterly. "One day everyone was smiling and we were talking about a new school and town hall, the next day—nothing! Just an empty bank and an empty hole in the mountain that we'd dropped a half million dollars into. The stock they issued isn't worth the ink that they used to print it."

Clint shrugged. "There's not much I can do for your town, Sheriff. But maybe I can save others from being bled to death."

"I'm going to help you," Sheriff Lane said. "I feel responsible for not sniffin' out them rats in the first place."

"No," Clint said, not really wanting the man to become involved. "This is your town. This is where you're needed."

"The hell it is! Are you forgetting that I'm out of a job?" Andy Lane's eyes became excited. "But if I was to help you arrest those three and recover some of the money, then I'd be a hero! I'd have a job for the rest of my days. I'd become mayor!"

Clint shook his head. "I really don't think it would be best if you came along."

"I'm comin' no matter what you think," Lane vowed. "Besides, the minute I spot any one of those three, I'll recognize 'em. That could be a hell of a big help for you, Gunsmith. It could save your bacon."

"But they'd also recognize you."

The Gunsmith could see by Lane's expression that he hadn't thought of it that way.

"Well," Lane said, "I'm out of work and a thousand dollars which was my life's savings. Now, I can stay here and clean spitoons or work some miserable little job even a boy could do, or I can try and grab the golden ring and make my own legend—just like you have."

Lane unpinned his badge and marched over to his rifle rack. There were two weapons, a double-barreled shotgun and an old Winchester with a broken stock which had been wrapped in rawhide. Lane removed both weapons.

"I think these are unloaded," he said, inspecting them. "And I don't believe I have any shells. Do you have any extra?"

Clint scowled. "A sheriff ought to keep his weapons in good order and always loaded."

"I know. I know. But my feeling is that, if a man has a loaded weapon, he's more inclined to use it."

Clint had to bite off a harsh comment and he managed to say, "I sure wish you'd reconsider going. I'll travel fast and . . ."

"On that big mule I saw you ride in on? Ha!"

Clint's cheeks stung with anger. "That mule will walk most any horse into the ground."

"I'm coming," Lane said, "with or without bullets."

"Great," Clint snapped, heading for the door. "Just great."

ELEVEN

Clint was furious about having Andy Lane join him in the search for Ben Towers and his two accomplices. The ex-sheriff of Madrid had, in Clint's opinion, been extremely fortunate to survive, given his decided reluctance to use force. If Lane had ever confronted a really bad man, he would have died years ago. And now the stubborn fool was convinced he could be helpful and perhaps even redeem himself.

"He probably can't even shoot straight," Clint groused as he found a good cafe and ordered a steak dinner.

The steak was tough and the potatoes were burned, but Clint wolfed them down because he was sick to death of his own poor trail cooking.

"Where can a man get some food to take out on the trail around here?"

"I'll sell you an apple pie for two dollars," the man who'd served him said hopefully.

"No thanks. I was thinking of flour, raisins and such."

"Down the street six doors is the Madrid General Store. They'll fix you up with whatever you need."

"Thanks," Clint said, paying his bill. "And maybe I will stop by for a pie just before I leave."

The man waved and Clint went down the street. The Madrid General Store was like a hundred others he'd seen in small frontier towns. It was cramped, packed with tin cans, blankets, boots, and jars of home canned fruits and vegetables. There were pickle and flour barrels and a shelf of medicines and bandages. Behind the scarred wooden counter was a collection of used guns, rifles, and a stack of ammunition.

Clint bought shotgun shells for Andy Lane. If he had to have the man along, it was best that he at least have a chance of intimidating someone.

"Comes to $18.75," the man behind the counter said, after laboriously adding and re-adding the figures.

Clint paid the man and told him to put everything except the ammunition into one gunnysack.

"You just passing through?" the storekeeper asked.

"Yep."

"You ought to stay around a while. We could use some new blood in Madrid."

"Not mine," Clint said, swinging the gunnysack over his left shoulder and heading out the door.

Andy Lane was sitting outside on the sorriest-looking horse Clint had ever seen. It was a dapple gray with a head like a keg of nails and feet as big around as plates. Its head was pointing at the ground, its eyes were closed and its lower lip was hanging loose as if it wanted a pinch of tobacco.

"You think you can keep up with me on that?" Clint asked, heading for his mule.

"Hell yes! He might not look like much, but he's a hell of a mover."

"Twenty years ago he might have been," Clint drawled, "but not anymore. Why don't you just take my advice and stay here."

"What for? I told you I was out of a job. But if I can help you nab Ben Towers and his two tricky friends, then I'm back in business."

Clint studied the man's outfit. The old Winchester and the shotgun were strapped to his saddle, barrels pointed to the ground.

"Don't you have any saddle scabbard for those things?"

"Nope."

"Is that your idea of a bedroll?" Clint asked, staring at the huge feather mattress and blankets that Andy had rolled up and tied down behind his cantle.

"A man out on the trail sure don't want to freeze or wind up stiff. And at my age, it's easy to do both," Andy said, his voice taking on a defensive edge. "You'll wish you had a mattress like mine on cold nights in the high Rockies."

Clint shook his head. "It's a marvel to me how you ever swung your leg over your saddle with that big thing. And what about food? I don't mean to feed you every step of the way."

"I'd not expect it of you," Andy snapped. "There's food wrapped up in the mattress and blankets. Some real good venison jerky. Salt pork. A sugared ham. A few bags of licorice and a couple jars of honey which is good for the digestion. I also got a few tins of jam and peaches, a couple bottles of brandy and . . ."

"What do you think we're going on!" Clint demanded. "A picnic? Andy, we're after hard, ruthless men."

The ex-sheriff's smile died. He sucked in his gut and puffed out his chest. "Don't you think I know that? You aren't the only one that's had to keep law and order."

Clint could see that further conversation was wasted. He tied everything securely on his saddle, then led Rusty on down to the cafe where he'd eaten less than twenty minutes earlier.

"What are you going to do now?" he asked. "Have another meal?"

"Nope."

Clint went inside and bought his apple pie. He was already eating it with his fingers when he walked back out the door.

"Jaysus," Andy Lane groused, "and to think that just a minute ago you was givin' me fits for bringing some decent vittles."

"Just keep your lip buttoned and we'll get along just fine," Clint said, balancing his pie as he untied his mule and climbed aboard.

As they rode out, Clint eating his apple pie and ex-sheriff Lane astride what Clint was certain had to be the ugliest horse in the entire Colorado Territory, Clint saw their reflections in the barber shop's big glass window.

He was shocked. They sure were a pathetic pair. Why, if a real killer like Ben Towers saw them right now, he'd probably laugh himself plumb to death.

Because they got a late start, they only covered about fifteen miles that afternoon before sundown. They camped along a fine stream where prospectors were panning for gold.

"You picked a poor stretch of water," a miner said, coming over to their campfire just after sundown. "My guess is that every rock and pebble, every damned grain of sand has been worked."

"We're not prospectors," Andy Lane said, looking up from the sugar ham he was devouring with more gusto than he'd shown all day.

"Well," the prospector snorted, "what be ya?"

"Lawmen," Lane said around a mouthful of ham. "And the Gunsmith and me figure to capture some real desperados."

Clint winced. The term "desperados" could only be found in the cheap dime novels that circulated in the West and were the cause of almost universal hilarity.

The prospector studied them both. "Well," he said after a long pause, "I just hope that them 'desperados' have a good sense of humor."

"Now what the hell is that supposed to mean!" Andy shouted as the man turned and staggered off with gales of whoops and laughter.

"Let it be," Clint said, feeding their fire and grateful for the cover of darkness.

Andy finished the entire ham in one sitting that night

and he even licked the muslin clean that it had come wrapped in.

"Brandy?"

Clint wanted to refuse but he was so dejected that he nodded his head. "Sure, why not."

Andy was delighted. He found a tin cup and poured generously. Raising the bottle, he said, "A toast to our adventure and to catching the desperados!"

"Don't *ever*," Clint warned, "call them desperados again."

"But . . . but why not!"

"Because that's just a dime novel term and I can't stand it."

"Why, because you've been written up in dime novels yourself?"

"Maybe."

Andy upended the bottle and stared at Clint across the flames. "You know, if I had your reputation, I'd sure enjoy life a lot more than you do. I'd have women hanging off my arms and I'd be ridin' a fancy carriage."

"Would you now."

"Yep. And I'd have a wild west show, like old Buffalo Bill only better." He frowned. "Please don't take this wrong, but you don't seem to be a very enterprising fella, Gunsmith."

Clint tossed his brandy down. "Let me tell you something," he said, stabbing his arm out with his empty glass for a refill. "Having a gunfighter's reputation is like having a bounty on your head. Everybody wants a piece of you. Kids hardly wet behind the ears think they can become famous with one lucky bullet. Shaking drunks who once had dreams that didn't work have one drink too many and decide they can die famous by killing a famous man. A gunfighter with a reputation can't trust anyone."

Andy refilled his glass and then took another long pull on the bottle. "I never thought of it quite that way," he admitted. "But I'd say that it's better to die famous than poor

and unknown and that's the way I'm going if I don't have
a hand in catching Ben Towers and those other two."

Clint could see that trying to talk sense into this man was
as meaningless as a belch in a blizzard.

"One thing we got to have," Andy said, "is some kind of
a plan on how to look for those fellas. You got one yet?"

"No."

Andy's bushy eyebrows shot up. "Well what was you
planning to do, just ride around these mountains until we
starve?"

"Hell no! I was fixing to ask questions in every town.
Sooner or later, I'd learn something from someone about
a new mining strike and maybe a stock issue. Ben Towers
and his two accomplices are running a game that takes a
lot of time and money. They can't play it and move around
very fast—but we can."

"But there's still hundreds of mining towns in Colorado,"
Andy argued. "Maybe we should split up and . . ."

"No! Be just my luck you'd find them first. They'd
probably shoot you but not before you ruined my own
game."

"Well hells bells! First you don't want me to come along,
now you don't want me to leave."

"Oh, you can leave if you promise to ride that jug-headed
horse on back to Madrid and stay there."

"No deal," Andy said, holding out the bottle to which
Clint's hand just naturally brought his cup for a third refill.
"You've got *your* glory, friend. I need a little for myself
now."

Clint drank and stared darkly into the fire. The brandy
was strong and he listened to wind singing through the
overhead pines. Across from him, Andy had pried open a jar
of strawberry jam and was spreading it on soda crackers.

Clint sighed. The man was a danger and the Gunsmith
was half of a mind to sneak out and leave him in the
night. Andy wouldn't be any better tracker than he was

sharpshooter, horseman or lawman. He'd give up and go
back to Madrid and take whatever kind of a job he could
find. It would be hard on his feelings but at least he would
probably live to his natural age.

"If you're thinking of skippin' out on me in the night,"
Andy said munching into his crackers and jam, "I won't
go back. I couldn't do that having been a man of respect
until now. So I'd keep riding and searching for the men
we're after and my chances of finding them are as good as
yours."

Clint tossed the rest of his brandy down and eased into
his bedroll without saying a word. One thing that seemed
pretty obvious to him was that his luck was still running
bad. What bigger fool than Andy Lane could he possibly
have hooked up with?

"Well," Andy said, hiccuping into the darkness. "Are you
gonna run out on me?"

"No," Clint growled. "But I'm going to get up before
sunrise and kick you out of that big damned mattress. We'll
break camp before the sun is off the mountaintops and you'd
better be ready if you're coming with me."

"I'll be ready," Andy vowed. "I need to find them even
worse than you do. By the way, why do *you* need to find
them?"

"It's a long story," Clint said, thinking of Miss Lucy
Mullane, Rosie, and James Mooney who was linked to
Ben Towers. "But a big part of it is the little girl. Her
real mother will give up anything to have her back."

"So *that's* it!"

"That's what?"

Andy chuckled and fingered the last of his jam from the
jar. "The mother, of course! You either want her body—or
her money—or both!"

Clint pushed his hat over his eyes and tried to go to
sleep.

"Well! Ain't you gonna even answer me?"

"Nope," Clint said quietly, "but if you don't shut up and let me sleep, I'm going to make you swallow that jam jar whole."

The ex-sheriff didn't say another word. He just smashed the jam jar into their campfire, eased down on his huge mattress, and went to sleep.

TWELVE

In the days that followed, Clint and Andy settled into what could best be described as peaceful coexistence. The Gunsmith quickly came to understand that Andy Lane was indeed a very fine, well-meaning fellow. And Clint, knowing he was Lane's model of the quintessential lawman, felt responsible for the older man's grandiose delusions.

"I want you to teach me the fast draw," Andy said on the third day that they were together. "I want to learn all the tricks of the trade."

Clint frowned. "I thought you told me that you opposed the use of weapons except as a very last resort."

"I do!"

"Then I think," Clint said, "you should respect your own feelings and stay away from firearms."

"But someday I may have to kill a man in a shootout," Andy protested. "In fact, I might even have to go to my guns when we find Ben Towers and those other two."

"I hope not," Clint said with utmost sincerity. "And if we do, the only chance you'd have would be to use that shotgun. At close range, it's a big equalizer."

Andy rode along in sullen silence for awhile. "Then I take it you're not going to teach me the fast draw?"

"That's right," Clint replied. "When it comes to handling a Colt, a little knowledge is far worse than none at all."

"You don't think much of me, do you," Andy groused.

Clint heard the injured pride in Andy's voice and he felt a rush of guilt.

"Look, Andy, I like you just fine. It's just that you ought to rethink what you want out of life. I've told you that a gunman's reputation can be a hard thing to live with. Seems to me that what you ought to be thinking about is settling down to a nice, peaceful life. Get married and have children. You strike me as the kind of man that ought to have a little business and family."

"Naw," he said, "I was never any good with women. They don't care much for me. I can't figure out why."

"You're just fine," Clint said. "You look respectable and you'd make a good catch for some pretty little gal."

"I'd like to think so," Andy said, "but women avoid me for some reason. Now, if I had me a reputation—if I could recover all that money they stole from Madrid, now that might change things around plenty."

Clint started to tell Andy that becoming a hero was fine but it didn't last very long. Sometimes a day, maybe even a week. After that, people just naturally wanted to know what you could do for them next.

"I need your help on this, Gunsmith," Andy said solemnly. "There's no way that I could catch, arrest and bring those three to justice all on my own."

"I think you're probably right," Clint said.

"Then you won't run out on me?"

"Naw," Clint said, "we'll catch and bring them all in together."

"Then don't you think you'd best teach me at least a little bit about the fast draw?"

"All right," Clint said, reining in his mule and dismounting. "Get down and we'll have a lesson."

"Right here and now?"

"Why not?" Clint looked around. They were on a lonely mountain trail with not a soul in sight. Just rocks, pines and a whole lot of bright blue sky.

"All right," Andy said, dismounting.

They tied their mounts to a little pine tree and Clint waited until Andy was standing beside him.

"The fast draw takes all your concentration," he began. "You can't be worried about dying or missing. You have to kind of block everything out except the target in front of you."

"Do you always aim for his heart, or sometimes do you just try and wing 'em?"

Clint shrugged. "Depends. If I judge a man to be good with a gun, I'll shoot to kill. But if he's drunk or wearing some old pistol that looks like it'll as likely blow his hand off as shoot me, then I'll try and wing him."

Andy nodded with approval. "That's what I'd try to do."

"Listen," Clint said angrily, "anytime *you* draw your gun, you'd best be aiming for the biggest part of a man—his chest. Only an expert would shoot to wing a man and you'll never be that good with a sixgun. Is that understood?"

"Why sure," Andy stammered. "I didn't mean to get you all riled."

Clint drew in a deep breath and let it out slowly. "I'm sorry I lost my temper," he said, "but I don't want your death to one day be on my conscience. So if you have to shoot at a man, I want you do shoot for the chest. Understood?"

"Sure."

"Now," Clint said, his hand shading his gunbutt, "watch."

In slow motion, he dropped his hand down on the butt of his Colt, thumbed back the hammer as he drew the weapon up, and the instant it was level, he fired.

"That don't look so hard."

"Oh yeah?" Clint asked, dropping his smoking gun back into his holster. "If you do that about ten thousand times, you might just get a little quick. Like this."

Now his hand flashed downward, and the gun seemed to stick to his hand as it came up and belched smoke and flame. From start to finish, the whole motion didn't take much more time than an eye blink. And twenty yards away, a pine cone exploded from its branch.

"Holy cow!" Andy exclaimed, his eyes round with wonder. "I never seen anything like that in my whole life!"

Clint didn't say anything. Ten years ago he'd been a shade faster, but he'd worked hard to compensate by improving his accuracy.

"Let me try it now," Andy said, pushing back his coat to reveal the scarred butt of a pistol resting in a holster that to Clint looked like it might have gone through the Civil War.

Andy crouched low.

"Don't bend your knees like you're getting ready to leap into a pond," Clint said.

Andy straightened and drew a long breath, but his right hand was shaking so badly that Clint moved off a couple of paces.

"Just take your time and go slow," Clint advised.

With exaggerated slowness, Andy reached down, wrapped his fingers one by one around his gunbutt, then eased it out, leveled the weapon and fired at the opposing mountainside.

"How was that?" he asked eagerly.

Clint was examining the gun. It appeared likely to misfire, maybe come apart in thousand pieces of flying metal. Clint moved off a little farther.

"Okay," he said, "now a bit faster."

Andy nodded. He wagged his short, chubby fingers over the gunbutt and then he stabbed downward. He yanked the gun up and fired before it was level. A bullet ricocheted off a rock right in front of them, tore a hole through the Gunsmith's pants leg, and ripped across his boot top before it clipped the little pine tree where their animals were tied.

Rusty jumped back and brayed in alarm.

"Dammit!" Clint exclaimed. "I told you to just go slow!"

"I'm sorry!"

Clint bent and examined his boot. The errant slug had torn the top almost in half. He cussed silently and then he pulled his pants leg back down over the ruined boot.

"That's enough of a lesson for one day," Clint said. "Let's see if we can find us another mining town and a hotel room tonight."

Andy Lane thought that was a fine idea. "I'm about out of food and drink," he said. "But I'll do fine on my feather mattress in the pines."

"Suit yourself," Clint told the man as he untied the braying mule and climbed into his saddle.

THIRTEEN

Bodine, Colorado, rested just over ten thousand feet up in the central Rocky Mountains. At that high altitude, the air was thin and crisp, the sky cobalt blue. Bodine was cupped in a valley surrounded by craggy, snowcapped peaks from which waterfalls shimmered down towering granite cliffs. Eagles soared majestically over Bodine Valley, always careful to stay just out of range of the miners' rifles.

"It looks just like all the others," Clint said, "only a little more prosperous."

Andy nodded. "I hope they got some good cafes and general stores. I'm so hungry I could eat my horse."

"You'd be doing the West a favor," Clint deadpanned.

"Aw, he isn't *that* ugly."

"Yes he is," Clint said, urging his mule on down the steep trail toward the town below.

They had stopped at enough towns now that Andy knew the drill. The first place they'd visit would be the sheriff's office, if there was one.

"You mind if I just went on over to that cafe just up the street a piece?" Andy asked. "My gut is growling like a tall dog."

"No, you go right ahead," Clint said, spotting the sheriff's office and easing Rusty into the brisk midday street traffic.

Clint dismounted and dropped his reins. He started to go

into the office but a miner who'd been watching him said, "Don't you think you'd better tie that damned mule?"

"Nope," Clint said, one boot up on the porch. "But if it bothers you, go ahead."

The miner blinked in confusion. "Well you can't just let that big sumbitch wander around here!"

"He'll stay put," Clint said, opening the sheriff's office door and removing his hat.

The sheriff was in his late forties with salt-and-pepper hair and a white mustache and eyebrows. There were deep lines in his tanned face, and his clothes and boots were spattered with mud. The man was sound asleep in his office chair, snoring in tandem with an old derelict locked in his only cell.

The derelict was beaten up and also spattered with mud. He and the sheriff, Clint thought, made real fine bed-fellows.

"Ahh-hem," Clint coughed gently, not wanting to startle the man. "Ahh, sheriff?"

The man awoke, one eye at a time. He gazed unseeing at the Gunsmith, knuckled his eyes and squinted. "Who the hell are you?" he asked, fumbling around on his desk for a pair of spectacles.

Clint waited until the man located his glasses. "My name is Clint Adams. Maybe you've heard of me."

"Nope. Should I have?"

"People also call me the Gunsmith."

Now the man seemed to finally come awake. "*You're* the Gunsmith?"

"That's right."

"Humph!" The sheriff sized Clint up from his torn pants leg to the Stetson he wore decorated with a bullet hole. "Well, Gunsmith, you seem to have fallen on hard times."

"You look a little hard used yourself, Sheriff."

The man chuckled. "Spent half of last night and all this morning hunting that prisoner you see locked up."

"What did he do?"

"Got drunk. Raped a Ute Indian woman and beat the hell out of one of my deputies."

"He sounds like a mean one."

"He is," the sheriff said. "Sober, he's the salt of the earth. A nicer fella you'd never meet. But when he gets drunk, it's like the devil climbs inside of him."

"I've seen it too many times," Clint said. "He's either got to stop drinking or you keep him behind bars. That kind will get crazy and kill you some day."

"Well," the sheriff said, introducing himself as Horace Barnes, "he almost killed my deputy last night and he tried to kill me. This time, the judge will send him to the territorial prison."

Clint nodded. "Mind if I have a chair?"

"Hell no! Why, it's just a real big honor having you in Bodine. Now what can I do for you today?"

Clint liked this man. He was direct and got right to the point. "I come looking for a trio of mine swindlers," he said. "One of them is Ben Towers."

"But Towers is . . ."

"No," Clint interrupted, "the man isn't dead yet."

"Are you sure?"

"Dead sure," Clint replied, and he told Barnes about the three and how they operated their mining swindle.

Throughout the telling, Barnes was quiet and listening closely. When the Gunsmith was finished, he said, "Well sir, I just don't know."

"What don't you know?"

"We did have three fellas come through town about two months ago. As a matter of fact, one of them said he was thinking about opening an assay office."

"Did he?"

"Nope. He asked a lot of questions about the mines hereabouts and I told him that we were doing pretty good and that we could always use another assayer. In fact, we only have one and he ain't too reliable."

Clint waited expectantly. "So what happened?"

"He and his three friends just stayed a few days and rode on. Kind of surprised me because I thought sure the man would stay seeing as he'd of had more business than he could handle."

Clint scowled. "I'm afraid this swindle works best in a town where the mines are running out and the people are a little desperate for a strike. Desperate enough not to be so careful about how they invest their money."

"Maybe so."

Clint climbed to his feet. "Do you have any idea where they might have gone? Any idea at all?"

"Nope." Barnes scratched at the stubble on his chin. "However, I did hear that Aquarius has a new bank and assay office. Surprising since the town is failing."

Clint's hopes soared. "That is surpising. And where is this Aquarius?"

"About fifty miles north of here," Barnes said. "Now the freighting road leaving town will take you there. You can't miss it."

Clint stuck out his hand. "I'm much obliged."

"Well good luck," Barnes said. "I suppose you're after a pretty big reward."

"My reward will be seeing Ben Towers back in prison or swinging from a rope," Clint said. "But there's other reasons as well."

"Why don't you stay the night and rest up? You can get an early start and be in Aquarius by tomorrow night."

Clint was mighty eager to reach Aquarius but, in truth, he was nearly played out and needed a good night's sleep in a real bed after a hot bath and a good feed.

"Maybe we will."

"We?" the sheriff asked.

"I've got friend riding along. His name is Andy Lane. He was the sheriff of Madrid. Maybe you've heard of him."

Barnes chuckled. "You don't want to hear what I've heard which is mostly how he doesn't want to use a gun and he can eat half a cow at a single sitting."

"That's him," Clint said with a wry grin.

"How'd you ever get stuck with a man like that?"

"Long story," Clint said. "And not worth the wind to tell it."

He left as soon as Barnes told him the best hotel, cafe and livery. Clint untied Andy's jug-head from the hitch rail and boarded both animals with orders to give them plenty of grain.

"You got a nice mule, mister," the liveryman said, "but the best thing I could give that sorry horse is a big dose of rat poison."

"Not my horse or my problem," Clint said. "Just feed and grain him. If his ugliness bothers you, keep him inside in a dark stall. But better keep my mule around him. The pair of them are starting to get attached."

"They'll do that," the man said as Clint left carrying his rifle, saddlebags and what supplies he did not trust leaving to the liveryman's care.

He found Andy already piling into a big plate of beans and potatoes. Clint joined the ex-sheriff and when they were through eating, he told Andy where their mounts were being boarded.

"Then that's where I'll bed down," Andy said.

"I'll be around first thing tomorrow morning," Clint told him as they parted. "Be ready to ride at daybreak."

That night, Clint had a long bath while his clothes were being laundered. He had also asked if the old woman who picked up his clothes knew of a good seamstress who could mend his bullet-torn pants leg.

"I know a lady who'll do it for three dollars."

The price was high but Clint agreed. After the laundry-woman was gone, the Gunsmith briefly considered going out to find a new pair of boots but decided that he could get by with those he was wearing. Besides, he had no clothes while they were being washed and ironed.

It was nearly ten o'clock at night when a knock sounded

on his door and Clint rolled off his bed, grabbed his gun and called, "Who is it?"

"It's Katie Woods."

"Who?"

"I'm the seamstress."

Clint went and opened the door, hiding behind it. "Give me the pants and I'll get your money," he said, surprised to see that the woman holding his pants was quite handsome, though a little hard around the mouth. She had long, brown hair tied in a bun and bold eyes.

"Money first and then the pants," she told him, holding the pants just out of reach and sticking out her hand, palm up.

"All right," Clint said, pushing the door not quite shut.

He went to his bedside dresser and found his wallet. Unfortunately, the smallest bill he had was ten dollars.

"You got any change for a ten?"

"Nope." The woman came inside. She studied Clint, who was standing in nothing but his underclothes. "I hear you're a famous man."

"News gets around fast in this town, doesn't it."

"You may be famous, but you're not rich, that's for sure. A lot of men wouldn't even bother to have these worn old pants mended. They'd just buy a new pair."

Her frankness rankled the Gunsmith. "Those pants have a few more miles in them."

Katie Woods shrugged. "I fixed them so you can hardly tell they were ripped. But they're getting a little shiny in the seat."

"What do you want to do about the change?" Clint said. "I'd go get some change but my shirts are being laundered. Should be back back before too long."

"I could wait." Katie looked around. "You got anything to drink, Gunsmith?"

"Just whiskey," he said, motioning toward a bottle on the bedside table.

"That's my favorite," she said brightly, tossing the pants

on the bed and snatching up the bottle. She uncorked it and took three long swallows.

"You drink like a man," he said.

Katie studied him intently. "Well if I do, that's *all* I do like a man."

Clint took the bottle and drank. "So what are we going to do about those pants, Katie?"

"Why don't I just keep your whole ten dollars," she said.

"That's a lot more than the pants are worth," he told her.

Katie was wearing a shawl and she flung it aside, then began to unbutton her blouse. Clint watched closely, and, when he saw how large and firm her breasts were he could not help but reach out, cup them gently, and kiss the woman's large brown nipples.

Katie pulled his face down between her breasts and reached for the Gunsmith's rising manhood. "Ten dollars and breakfast," she whispered in his ear.

Clint nodded, pushed her onto the bed, pushed her dress up around her hips, slipped his forefinger into her womanhood, and began to wiggle it around until Katie's ripe body began to respond.

"You don't believe in messing around much, do you?" Katie panted as the Gunsmith stood up and removed his underpants, then climbed between her legs with his rod as stiff as a flagpole.

"It's been awhile," Clint said, pushing Katie's dress up even higher as he shoved his throbbing rod into her wetness. "It's been a damned long while!"

Katie groaned with pleasure and her heels began to rake the bedding as Clint worked over her. She pulled his face to her breasts. When he began to nip her large nipples, her body started to quiver.

"Take it easy," Clint panted, "we got a long way to go."

But Katie didn't. She squealed with joy and her thighs

locked around Clint's plunging hips as she lost control of herself.

The Gunsmith growled low in his throat and with several more powerful thrusts, he exploded into her body and filled her with his seed.

That night Clint made love until he was sore and spent. Long before daylight, he tiptoed outside to find his laundered clothes stacked neatly beside his door. He dressed quickly in the darkness, then left ten dollars beside the sleeping seamstress.

"You make love even better than you make a stitch," he said with a tender smile.

She opened her eyes. Moonlight streamed through their open window. "What are you doing?" she asked with alarm.

"I have to go."

"Can't it wait!" she asked.

"I'm sorry. I wish it could. I could make love to you until I'd driven myself to a nubbin' and never complain."

She smiled and reached for him but Clint stepped away.

"Goodbye," he said.

"What about that breakfast you promised."

"Another time," he said, backing out the door and closing it softly behind.

On his way to find Andy Lane, it occured to the Gunsmith that Aquarius was only fifty miles away and that maybe—just maybe—it would prove to be the end of this long but eventful search for Ben Towers and Lucy Mullane's missing child.

FOURTEEN

It was raining the day that they left for Aquarius. The sky just opened up and it poured. Clint and Andy had not ridden ten miles before they came to a swollen stream traversed by a crude log bridge that was very nearly being breasted. The logs were shaking and white water was pounding and foaming.

"It looks bad!" Clint shouted into the rain as water sluiced off his hat brim. He urged the mule forward, and Rusty snorted with alarm. He placed his two front hooves on the bridge, felt it shiver, and jumped back, braying in protest.

"Come on!" Clint said, whipping the mule with his reins. "We can't just stay here."

But the mule went stubborn. Clint slashed it several more times, but the animal's resolve not to cross seemed to solidify. It leaned back, front legs braced, and would not budge.

"Ha!" Andy said, whipping his old horse forward. "That's what you get for riding one of them damned stubborn things."

The horse didn't like the feel of the shaky log bridge any better when he stepped onto it, but Andy drove him forward. "Come on! Let's show them how to get things done!"

Clint dismounted and tried to pull the mule onto the bridge, but the obstinate critter rolled its big brown eyes in fear and brayed right into his face. The wind-driven rain was coming down in sheets, and the pine forest was swaying like prairie wheat in the face of a tornado.

The Gunsmith was cussing and pulling when he heard a cry. Turning around so suddenly he almost slipped and fell in the mud, Clint saw the logs began to separate just as Andy and his jug-headed horse reached the middle of the torrent.

"Go!" Clint shouted, dropping his own reins and leaning forward. "Go!"

But Andy and his horse seemed to freeze in terror. Clint looked on with horror as the logs were torn apart, sending man and horse into the raging water.

"Help!" Andy cried before he went under.

Clint saw the old horse roll right over the ex-sheriff and then slam into a boulder. The force of the water was so strong that the animal lifted completely out of the water on impact, then was sucked down into the current and spun away.

"Andy!"

Though it would have been impossible for Andy to see or hear him, the man's head appeared. Clint caught a glance of a face white with fear and then Andy went boiling over rocks, bobbing like a cork.

The Gunsmith began to race down the riverbank, shouting hoarsely into the wind and the heavy, rumbling thunder. Slipping and falling, almost going into the river himself, he tore through thickets that left big welts on his face. Clint tumbled over slick rocks and twisted his ankle in a crevass, but he kept going until he saw Andy smash into a boulder, then lift under the mighty current, to be hurled into a tangle of snared brush, branches, and limbs.

The man was unconscious. Clint saw blood seeping from a deep laceration along the line of his jaw.

"Andy!" Clint shouted, edging as far into the water as he dared and finding he was still a good two yards short. "Andy!"

The man didn't respond. Clint inched forward, and the current started to tear away his footing. He surged backward an instant before he would have been swept away.

Shivering and soaked, Clint watched helplessly, knowing that the tangle of debris that had caught Andy might be torn away at any minute and swept downriver.

The Gunsmith wasn't a cowboy and he didn't have a rope, but he did have a pair of rope reins, so he raced back upriver to the mule which hadn't moved. He unbridled the mule and ran back to Andy. Looping the bridle over a solid rock, he tied a rein around his upper arm and inched back out into the torrent. The wind was shrieking now and the river was rising every minute. Clint kept inching forward. When he felt his feet start to lift from the riverbed, he lunged at Andy, grabbed his coat, and felt the debris give way.

The next few moments were chaos, as the Gunsmith clung to Andy, fought the current, and inched his way back to the shore. It seemed to take years but somehow he got the man to the muddy bank and dragged him up into the thickets, under a rock, and out of the rain.

Andy had a pulse, but it was feeble and racing. Clint left him and ran back to the mule.

"Come on!" he shouted, pulling its head around and finally getting it into motion.

The mule allowed itself to be led downriver. Clint pulled it in close to the rocks where Andy was still lying unconscious.

The Gunsmith found dry matches, and there was enough wood under the rock shelter to get a fire going. It took another quarter of an hour to feed enough life into the fire to cause his clothes to steam.

By sundown he had scavenged more at least semidry wood under the bigger rocks, and Andy was conscious again, though he acted dazed.

"Jeezus," he whispered, "I feel like I been brought back from the dead."

"You look it, too," Clint said, "though I suppose I don't look a hell of a lot better."

Andy was so shaken by his near death that he'd even lost his appetite. "I saw a light," he said. "And I saw myself under that river, hung up on a limb way down deep."

"Aw, come on now," Clint said, not wanting to hear this.

"It's true!" Andy insisted. "Everything was real bright and I wasn't cold or afraid anymore. I just looked at my body snagged on that limb under all that water and I said to myself that I was leaving this world."

"Well," Clint snapped, his own body badly bruised by the ordeal, "I guess that you were called back to earth for some reason or other."

"Sure I was!" Andy said, warming his pale hands over the fire, "I was brought back because I was meant to be famous some day. I was meant to be the hero of Madrid."

Clint stared up at the man. Andy was a complete mess. He looked worse than any loser in a barroom brawl that the Gunsmith had ever seen.

"Andy, you've got some real nasty lumps on your head. I think you're just talking a little crazy."

"No I'm not," the man insisted. "I was meant to gun down Ben Towers."

Clint groaned. He stuck his hand out from under the rocks and gave the mule a handful of raisins. "It stopped raining. This river will probably be a creek by morning that we can cross."

But Andy wasn't listening. He kept insisting that he'd been saved because he was destined to be the one that either killed or captured Ben Towers. Clint listened to the man's ravings until dusk settled in; then he fed the fire up as high as he dared and fell asleep.

In the morning, the sky was blue and cloudless. And true to Clint's prediction, the angry river had subsided into a gentle stream. Everything would have been fine except that Andy kept mourning the loss of his horse and Clint was so stiff from his bruises that he had trouble walking.

"Aquarius is going to seem like a hundred miles away before we reach it," Clint said.

Andy was in a far more optimistic frame of mind. Now convinced his life had been spared for some great destiny, he hobbled out from under the rocks heedless of his own cuts and bruises and proclaimed it to be a fine day.

"I can always buy another horse and mattress," he said, following Clint and his mule across the stream.

"And once I'm famous for killing or capturing Ben Towers, someone will probably write a dime novel about me, same as they have you."

"I never saw a penny off one of them," Clint groused.

"Aw, it ain't the money I'm looking forward to," Andy said. "It's the respect and the way that the women will treat me."

Clint didn't feel obliged to make any comments on the subject. With his body half-purple from the pounding he'd taken to save Andy, he felt awful. His hat had been lost in the river and his boots, already worthy of the junk pile, were a sodden mass of squishing leather.

"I got twenty-five dollars left in my pockets," the Gunsmith announced. "And I'm going to gamble it up to over a hundred as soon as we reach the poker tables at Aquarius."

"What! How can you say that seeing as how Ben Towers and his three men might be in that very same town?"

"Because," Clint said, "I'm not going to face Towers looking like a damned ragamuffin. And besides, I lost my sixgun in the water when I was trying to get you unhooked."

"You didn't even remove your holster?" Andy said, shocked by this bit of news.

"You were about to be swept away again," Clint said. "I was too occupied thinking about how I was going to get you to shore to worry about my gun."

"I do owe you my life," Andy said, "but what good will you be to us if you're unarmed?"

Right then and there, Clint almost went for the fool's throat. Instead, he kicked the mule and Rusty brayed with his own sufferings as they continued on toward Aquarius. All that the Gunsmith was thinking about was his luck. It had kept going downhill for as long as he cared to remember. And now, all beaten up, without a gun and with just a few borrowed dollars left, it was time to sit down at a poker table and go for broke.

And if he lost everything—then at least he'd know that his luck was still running rotten and that the best thing he could do was go after Ben Towers with Andy's damned old shotgun.

FIFTEEN

By the time that Clint and Andy Lane reached Aquarius, the skies had darkened again and were threatening rain. The two men had alternated all day long between riding the mule and walking, and by the time they reached their destination they were both covered with mud and staggering with fatigue. For that matter, the mule looked worn out as it shambled patiently along with its head down. Clint believed there was now a sullenness in its large brown eyes.

Because he had grown rather fond of the animal and attributed the fact that he and Andy had not drowned to its good sense, Clint used three dollars of his money to make sure that Rusty had the best stall, the cleanest dry straw, and the richest hay and grain obtainable.

"What's so special about that ugly old mule?" the livery-man asked as Clint and Andy were starting to leave.

"He saved my life," Clint said, "and that made it possible for me to save my friend's life."

"Hump," the liveryman grunted, too dull or incurious to pursue the issue.

"You called me your 'friend,' " Andy said happily. "And I didn't even think you liked me."

"Oh, I like you just fine," Clint said, hearing the distant sound of thunder and noticing a weathered gallows they passed with a hangman's frayed noose waving in the stiffening breeze. "It's just that you worry me some."

Andy looked up at the Gunsmith, his eyes were joyful in his otherwise battered face. "I'm honored that you worry about me."

"Some I do," Clint admitted, "but mostly I'm worried that you're going to do something that might get me killed."

Andy blinked and blustered to cover his injured pride. "Well you don't have to worry about that any! I can take care of myself and believe me, I'll do my share. In fact, I think that *you're* the one that is the bent spoke in the wheel."

Clint planted his ruined boots down solidly, grabbed the man and hauled him up by the shirtfront. "Now listen you," he growled, "I almost got drowned trying to save your worthless life! And as for helping me to kill or capture Ben Towers, why the very thought of you interfering gives me the shakes."

Clint pushed the man away from him. "Here!" he snapped, pulling ten soggy dollars out of his pocket. "You can have this if you agree to stay out of sight until I check this town out."

"I wouldn't take your money if I was starving!"

Clint wanted in the most god-awful way to smash Andy in the face, but he couldn't. Andy Lane's round, bland face was already all cut up and besides, the fool was ignorant, not malicious.

"This is where we're parting the blanket," Clint said. "You have taxed my patience too far this time. And I want you to stay the hell out of the way until I've either got Ben Towers and his friends behind bars, or I'm sure that they aren't operating in this town."

"Fat damn chance," Andy said, gripping his shotgun. "I know the law as well as you do and you can't keep me off the streets. It's a free country."

Clint had to force himself to turn and walk away real sudden or he'd have inflicted serious damage on Andy, beaten-up face or not. The Gunsmith headed for a barber and a bathhouse up the street. Then he aimed to buy himself a new set of clean clothes and a pair of boots. After that, he was going to take whatever money remained and play some poker. Maybe that wasn't too smart considering the way his luck was running, but sometimes a man had to force his luck to run good.

Three hours later Clint was clean, barbered, and working his toes in a pair of plain but serviceable boots. They weren't new boots, but the man who'd worn them last had died in a gunfight and he'd polished the boots the night before he'd died.

But most important of all, Clint had a stack of money in front of him and he was winning at cards. They were playing poker, a dollar ante and nothing wild. The game suited Clint just fine. He was equally good at poker or faro, and if his luck was even average he almost always walked away from the tables a winner.

"Well, stranger," a man said to the Gunsmith, "you're up on us about thirty-five dollars. I expect you're having a pretty good run of luck for so early in the evening."

The Gunsmith nodded agreeably. He knew that despite the haircut, shave and clean clothes he still looked a little rough because of all his scratches and the welts he'd taken while racing back and forth along the riverbank saving Andy.

"You don't talk much, do you?" another man said.

"I come to play and to win," Clint said, shoving two dollars forward and raising the bet.

Two of the five men met the raise and called.

"Four kings," Clint said, dropping his cards down on the table.

The other men scowled and tossed in their hands. It was the biggest pot yet, and the the Gunsmith raked in another twelve dollars. It wasn't the kind of a game that anyone was going to get rich at or lose their shirt, but Clint figured he could pick up a hundred dollars if his luck held until midnight. Then he'd go up to the room he'd taken and get a long overdue night's sleep. Tomorrow, he'd see the town sheriff and find out if his luck had really changed for the better and he'd finally overtaken Ben Towers.

But twenty minutes later they all heard gunfire up the street and when Clint instinctively gripped the arms of his chair to rise, one of the players said, "Don't mind that ruckus. Probably just some drunk miner trying to hit the wolf in the moon."

Clint relaxed. "I imagine your sheriff or a deputy will take care of that. Firing bullets in town can be dangerous."

"Hell," another player drawled, "Aquarius ain't got any law no more. Last sheriff we had got drunk and fell off his horse tryin' to rope a damned dog. Broke his fool neck and died two days later."

"Dumb bastard," another man said in agreement. "I'll see you two dollars and raise you five."

Clint was holding another very good hand and trying to concentrate on his cards. "I'll see that raise and raise you another five dollars."

All but two of the players folded and when Clint slapped down a ten-high straight, he heard groans and raked in the biggest pot of the night.

"I never seen your kind of luck," one of the losers carped.

"Well," Clint said, "I sure haven't been spending any good luck the past few months. Maybe it's all been saving up for tonight."

"Then maybe," came the unhappy reply, "I'll deal myself out of this game before I piss away a week's wages."

"Me too," another said.

Clint was about to try and change their minds when a man come bursting through the doorway.

"There's been a shoot-out down the street!"

"Anybody we know?" someone in the saloon asked.

"Yeah, that new banker, Mr. Boron. He was eatin' his steak and this beat-up lookin' sonofabitch pulled an old gun outa this holster that you wouldn't have worn to a Mexican cock fight and . . ."

Clint didn't hear the rest. He was out of his chair, scooping up his winnings to shove into his pocket and running toward the door with his Winchester clenched in his fist.

It was darker than the bowels of hell on the main street but down at the east end of town there were already a lot of people gathered outside with lanterns. Gimped up and in considerable pain, Clint did not break any speed records as he hobbled down the street praying that poor Andy hadn't gotten himself killed.

"Make way!" Clint shouted roughly as he knocked the spectators aside until he was kneeling in the dirt next to Andy.

The unlikely ex-sheriff who'd wanted to become a legend had been shot in the chest. In the flickering lamplight, Clint saw bright red blood pumping from Andy Lane's punctured lung and heard the too-familiar, ominous gurgles of a dying man. Andy's eyes were open, and he was staring up at the people holding lanterns.

"Someone get a doctor!" Clint shouted, knowing that a doctor would be powerless to save Andy's life.

The ex-sheriff gripped Clint's arm and when he spoke, bloody froth appeared on his lips. "Gunsmith, I should have listened to you!" he said urgently. "Should have listened."

"Who shot you, Andy?"

"The banker. I spotted him inside eating and tried to arrest him. But he had a derringer. I never even saw the damned thing until it was in his hand."

Andy coughed and a fine bloody mist sprayed Clint's new clothes. He didn't care. "You just wouldn't listen to me," Clint said gently. "Had to be a hero."

"I'm a fool, not a hero."

"You're a hero," Clint whispered, leaning closer. "I'll make sure that the people of this town know that it was *you* that protected whatever money that they'd have lost to the man."

Andy's face lit up. Positively glowed. "You will?"

"Sure. Did you see . . ."

"No." Andy closed his eyes and his head rolled back and forth. "But they're here. I'm sure of it. I can feel . . . ugggh!"

"Andy!"

But it was too late. Andy Lane heaved a deep sigh with his last breath and died. There was a long, long silence. Thunder rolled, a few drops of rain smattered the already muddy street before someone cleared his throat and said, "You gonna pay to bury him?"

Clint looked up suddenly and his face shocked the man who quickly stepped back in fear.

"I'll pay," Clint grated. "And so will that banker that shot him. He's a swindler."

"You got any proof of that?"

Clint pried the old sixgun out of Andy's hand. It was just a big, worn-out old Colt but at the sight of it everyone recoiled.

"This is all the proof I'll need tonight," Clint said. "Now which way did the that murdering bastard run?"

SIXTEEN

With Andy's old gun clenched in his fist, Clint hobbled down the street. He learned that the so-called banker was staying at the Embassy Hotel and that, as luck would have it, that establishment was at the opposite end of town.

The Gunsmith was nearly out of breath by the time he reached the Embassy, and Clint must have looked pretty intimidating, because the desk clerk tried to bolt and run when he barged into the lobby.

"Hold it!"

"Don't shoot me!" the man squealed, coming to a halt and throwing his hands into the air. "Please don't shoot me!"

"Which room is that banker staying in!"

"You mean Mr. Boron?"

"That'd be him. What room?"

"Two ten."

Clint glanced at the stairway. "Is he rooming with some-one posing as an assayer or a mining engineer?"

The desk clerk, a skinny man with a yo-yoing Adam's apple, stammered, "I . . . I can't say!"

"Sure you can," the Gunsmith said, cocking the old Army Colt.

"All right! All right! He's alone."

"You're sure?"

The desk clerk was sweating profusely. "Yes sir!"

Clint drew a deep breath and headed for the stairway. He wasn't at all sure that he could believe the desk clerk and it was damned important to know if he might run into all three of the men he sought upstairs.

Taking the stairs two at a time, Clint swiftly reached the top landing. The upstairs hallway was dim and carpeted. When the Gunsmith reached room 210, he pressed his ear to the door and listened intently. He could hear someone banging around inside, but no voices.

The Gunsmith wrapped his left hand around the door knob and slowly turned it. Locked! He stepped back, debating whether to shoot the lock apart or attempt to kick the door from its hinges. Locks could be impossible to shoot apart, so the Gunsmith reared back and kicked the door with all of his might. Wood splintered and the door buckled inward, but the lock and the hinges were strong enough to hold.

Damnation!

Clint cussed and kicked again. The door splintered even further but still did not break. Clint heard the familiar cock of a gun's hammer and jumped aside an instant before a slug ate its way through the door, missing him by inches. He jumped aside as two more bullets ripped through the door.

"Come out with your hands up or I'll kill you!" Clint shouted.

Another bullet was his answer and Clint pressed against the wall thinking that the man inside had one bullet left in his gun, two at the most—unless he had other weapons, which was plenty likely.

A full minute passed in silence and Clint knew that he had to act. He jumped back out in front of the door and booted it savagely. As the door crashed inward, the Gunsmith dropped to the floor, thumbing back the hammer of his sixgun and unleashing a bullet that passed unimpeded through an open window.

The room was empty.

Clint jumped up and ran to the window. He peered down into the alley to see a man hobble around the corner of the hotel and vanish. Clint spun around and started for the door. He was halfway across the room when someone holding a sixgun stepped into the open doorway. It happened so fast that the Gunsmith reacted on instinct. He threw himself behind the bed and heard the crash of guns and glass.

Clint pushed under the bed and fired at a pair of boot tops. The man in the doorway screamed and began firing into the mattress. Clint shoved his gun up and fired blindly, his bullets spaced so closely together that their report was like a single roll of thunder. When the hammer of his gun fell on an empty cylinder, the man in the doorway pitched forward, and his head struck the wooden floor just inches from Clint's smoking Colt.

Stuck under the bed, Clint stared into the glazing eyes of what he imagined was the bogus assayer. A pool of blood began to expand from under the man, and Clint saw his hand twitch as he tried to pull the trigger.

Clint tried to retreat but his belt hooked up on the underside of the box springs and he was stuck for a minute. Unable to back out, he had no choice but to go forward. That meant he'd have to practically climb over the dying man.

"Who was in here?" he asked, not really expecting an answer.

The man's lips moved silently.

"You were the assayer, weren't you?"

"Yes!"

"Where is Ben Towers?"

The man's lips twisted into a death grin and he said curses with his dying breath. Clint wiggled forward, shoving the dead man aside. He snatched the man's gun up, jammed it behind his belt, and staggered back out into the hallway and down the stairs.

The desk clerk was gone but there were several men gathered at the front door. Clint crashed into them, struck a post with his shoulder, and ran around to the alley following the man who'd jumped from his hotel window. But it was too dark to see anything.

Clint cussed inwardly and headed for the nearest livery stable. The banker would realize the game was up and he'd be bent on escape. To do that, he'd need a horse.

When the Gunsmith entered the nearest livery, there wasn't a sound except the low and strengthening rumble of a watchdog.

"Excuse me," Clint said, backing away from the livery barn and heading on down the street.

There were only three livery stables in Aquarius. His own mule was in one of them, and that was where the Gunsmith was headed now. Fortunately, it was close by. When Clint arrived he could tell there was a lantern glowing inside the barn, because he could see light through the cracks in the walls and around the big swinging barn doors.

Clint tiptoed to the door. He could hear voices arguing inside. Just as he was about to throw open the barn door he heard a loud grunt, followed by the heavy thud of what sounded like a man's body as it struck the dirt floor.

"Hold it!" Clint shouted, jumping inside.

There were three men. Clint had one split second to see the liveryman lying facedown on the dirt floor and two men standing over him with drawn guns. Clint fired and saw one of the men stagger, but before he could swing his gun and shoot again, the taller of the pair shot first.

Clint felt no pain but he did see a huge explosion of fire behind his eyes. His legs buckled, and he pitched forward as a second bullet slashed his shoulder. There may have been a third gunshot, but its sound was rushing off like a train speeding away into the night, leaving in its wake only darkness and desolation.

The Gunsmith was slapped into wakefulness and dragged to his feet by an angry mob.

"He killed the assayer and the liveryman!" someone yelled out to a crowd gathering in the street. "We ought to hang him!"

Clint felt himself being dragged outside. His head was throbbing so painfully that he couldn't think. He tried to focus but saw double.

"Get a rope!" someone shouted. "There's bound to be some in the barn."

Clint shook his head in a desperate effort to clear away the cobwebs in his mind.

"Mister," someone choked, spewing his foul breath into Clint's face, "you're gonna find out in about two minutes that the people of Aquarius don't put up with cold-blooded killers! No sir! We know how to hand out rope justice!"

Someone sucker-punched Clint in the gut and he doubled up and collapsed to his knees. A moment later, he felt a noose tighten around his neck.

"Get him up on that wagon! Drag it under that big tree."

Clint felt himself being lifted up and thrown into a wagon bed. Moments later, he was hauled to his feet and held upright.

"You got any prayers to make, make 'em now!"

Clint clenched his teeth together. He wasn't going to waste his last breath giving these people the satisfaction of an explanation. They were a murdering mob. Even if his head had been clear, he couldn't have made them see the truth.

The rope tightened around his throat, and Clint lashed out with his boot. He felt it connect solidly with flesh and heard a man cry in pain. Clint began to flail, half-blinded with pain, and he must have done a pretty good job because several more were knocked off the wagon before they were able to pin his arms behind his back and tie them together.

"I'm gonna take a hell of a lot of pleasure in helping yank this wagon out from under you," someone hissed.

Clint was suddenly alone on the wagon, and he knew the rope was in place. His lips pulled back from his teeth and he shouted, "You fools got the wrong man!"

Men shouted and jeered and Clint felt the wagon began to move under his feet. He walked with it to the end of the wagon bed and squeezed his eyes shut, steeling himself to die. He prayed that his neck would be broken but feared that he might be strangled instead.

I will jump up and drop, he thought.

"Hold it! Hold it!" Two gunshots split the night like a wedge.

"It's the liveryman!"

"You got the wrong man," a voice cried. "He ain't the one that hit me, boys, that's the Gunsmith!"

The hammering in Clint's ears during the next few moments was the sound of his own heart.

"Aw hell," a man finally growled. "Let's cut him down."

Clint felt the noose loosen. His legs buckled, and he pitched headfirst off the wagon, almost breaking his neck.

SEVENTEEN

"Ben," the man pleaded as he clung to a wooden fence behind Medgar's Mercantile. "Ben I can't go much farther. I'm bleeding to death! I got to see the doc!"

Ben Towers glanced sideways at his wounded companion. Wilkinson Ward, son of a banker and a famous Abilene prostitute, was dying. Now, the problem was simply how best to salvage what had been the beginnings of a very profitable venture here in Aquarius.

"I'm telling you!" Ward cried. "If you don't get me to a doctor, I'm going to die!"

Ward's aristocratic face was pinched and bone-white in the pale moonlight. He looked like walking death, and his eyes pleaded for help.

"We can't go to the doctor," Ben said quietly. "They'll be taking that liveryman to the doctor and he'll finger us for sure. The game is up. We should have killed him after I shot down the Gunsmith."

The bogus banker stared up at him. "It was the Gunsmith that shot me?"

"Yeah. I didn't recognize him until he was down."

Ward groaned and folded to his knees. "I don't care who he was! I got to see the doctor!"

Ben knelt at the man's side and slipped his arm around Ward's shoulder. For a moment, Ward thought the gunfighter was going to comfort him. Lift him up and carry

him if necessary to the doctor. But that illusion lasted only a
moment. Ward felt a searing pain in his gut and felt himself
being lifted from his knees as Ben Towers ripped the blade
of his Bowie knife upward.

Ward's eyes bugged. His mouth formed a large circle,
and a silent cry filled his mouth as he raised his hands,
reaching for Towers's throat. But his hands grew as heavy
as stone. As he died, he screeched, "Murderer!"

Ben rolled the body over and yanked his Bowie knife
free. He wiped the blade clean on Ward's fine coat and
emptied the man's pockets: gold watch, almost a hundred
dollars in cash, and the key to their new bank.

Ben Towers hurried up the street, cutting from alley to
alley until he slipped around to the front of the bank. Down
the street near the livery, he saw a big crowd. There must
have been fifty men with lanterns, and they seemed to be
gathered about a wagon.

Ben wondered about that, but he had not time to investi-
gate. Wilkinson Ward had heard gunshots from his upstairs
room, and it wasn't hard to guess that their assayer friend
had been shot down by the Gunsmith. And even though the
Gunsmith was now dead, there would be a run on their little
bank in the morning and the entire scheme they'd become
so adept at playing would quickly be exposed.

Ben opened the door to their bank and hurried to the
vault. How much money had they attracted from the towns-
people of Aquarius so far? Not much.

The safe was massive. Scarred from years of being
hauled from one boom town to the next, it was a relic
made in Baltimore and freighted into the Rocky Mountains
at least twenty years earlier. It weighed almost a thousand
pounds, and its door was a good four inches thick of solid
steel. The damn thing was built to appear indestructible. In
actuality, the combination had just three numbers, and its
tumblers were so worn that it practically opened whenever
the dial was spun in the proper sequence, regardless of
the numbers.

Ben had it open in less than a minute. He scooped out the cash and relocked the safe and the door on his way back outside. In the morning, someone would find Wilkinson Ward's body where he'd died in the alley. A hue and cry would bring the town running and that would be followed by a run on this bank by its new depositors. It might take days before the ugly little safe was violated and the theft discovered.

Once outside, Ben started to turn up the street, but then he stopped and looked back at the big crowd. What the hell was going on?

Curiosity drew him toward the crowd. He stayed on the boardwalk, a man apart and completely unnoticed. Suddenly, he saw the Gunsmith being hoisted onto a buckboard wagon with a hangman's noose around his neck.

Ben froze in the shadows. He blinked to make sure that his eyes were not betraying him, for he had been certain that he'd killed the famed gunman. But there the Gunsmith stood swaying as he faced his angry executioners. Wounded, of course—but very much alive.

"Strangle him," Ben hissed in a low voice.

But then the liveryman staggered out of his barn shouting that the Gunsmith was innocent. Ben cursed as the crowd listened and then spared the Gunsmith's life.

Slipping back into the shadows, Ben's mind raced. Everything had gone to hell in a handbasket, and just when they were ready to salt the mine and reel in the suckers! And the worst part of it was, the Gunsmith was still alive and would hound him until one of them were dead.

Ben Towers wasn't a runner and his natural instincts told him to kill the Gunsmith before he left Aquarius. Kill the man now while he was hurt and therefore most vulnerable. Kill him now and be the hunter instead of the hunted.

Ben watched as the Gunsmith was carried down to Doc Tarver's office. Satisfied, Ben headed for the nearest saloon and ordered himself a drink.

"A lot of excitement tonight, isn't there," he commented drily to the bartender.

"Sure is!"

Within an hour, the saloon was filled with men, all of them speculating about the recent gunfight.

"They say that the fella that was shot in the head is the Gunsmith. You believe that?" a man asked.

"Could be," Ben said.

"Well if it was, then he was probably trying to collect a bounty or something. Too bad he failed."

"Yes," Ben said, "but sooner or later, even the best have to fall."

The man looked at him strangely, wondering why Ben was smiling, and then he moved away to join his other friends.

Ben waited, feeling relaxed and confident as he sipped whiskey and water, listening to the crowd. He thought about all the stories he'd heard of the Gunsmith and remembered seeing the famous lawman in action once down in El Paso. Clint Adams was fast, too fast to challenge unless a man decided to wind up a dead fool. That's why it was important to kill him right now while he was probably doctored up with laudanum or whiskey to kill the pain.

"Going to be damned exciting when this whole thing unravels, isn't it, Mister."

Ben turned toward the young miner who had addressed him. The kid couldn't have been eighteen years old and he was swaying a little on his feet, drunk and too excited to go to bed and sleep.

"Yeah, it is," Ben said.

"Who you figure it was good enough to get the drop on a famous man like the Gunsmith?"

"I don't know," Ben said, "but I would expect he'd tell us all tomorrow morning."

"I'm so excited I can't hardly wait," the miner said. "I've heard about the Gunsmith for years but I never thought I'd ever have the chance to see him in person."

"He's just a man," Ben said. "Just a man like all the rest of us."

"No he ain't," the kid argued. "The Gunsmith is a legend. He's as famous as Wild Bill Hickock, Wyatt Earp or any of them fellas. And you know what?"

"What?"

"I'm going to ask him for his autograph tomorrow! Think he'll give it to me?"

"If he lives, he might."

The kid blinked. "What do you mean 'if he lives'?"

"Well," Ben said, unholstering his gun and reloading the two spent shells he'd fired at the Gunsmith, "it's just that a lot of things can go wrong for a man in the night. Even a man like the Gunsmith."

"What the hell kind of talk is that!" the kid demanded, his voice confused and becoming angry.

"Never mind," Ben said, easing his sixgun down into his custom-made holster and striding off toward the doctor's office.

EIGHTEEN

Clint grimaced as Dr. Tarver probed at the bullet crease in his scalp. "Am I going to live?"

"You are," the doctor said as he finished his examination. He found a roll of gauze and began to bandage the wound, wrapping it turbanlike around Clint's head. "I want you to stay the night."

Clint thought of Ben Towers. "I don't think I'd better do that," he said, standing up and suddenly feeling very dizzy.

"Stay down," the doctor said roughly. "You're in no condition to go anywhere."

With his head pounding and spinning like a top, Clint had to agree. He relaxed on the examining table. "What am I supposed to do, lie on this damned thing all night?"

"No," Tarver said, "I'll help you over to that cot by the rear wall. But you've got to promise to stay flat tonight."

"But what if I have to take a piss?"

"Hold it," the doctor said. "And I'm going to wait until morning to decide if that scalp of yours needs stitching."

"They wouldn't be the first."

"Are you still having moments of double vision?"

"Yes."

"I'm afraid that you're going to need a lot of rest because you've most likely got a concussion."

"From a bullet crease?"

"Why sure," the doctor said. "You've got to figure the impact that slug had against your skull. And you sure didn't help things when you landed on your head after taking a dive off that buckboard."

Clint felt his rope-burned neck and shuddered to remember how close he'd come to being hanged. "I guess now I know how it feels," he said, more to himself than the doctor.

"You *almost* know how it feels," Dr. Tarver amended. "That salve I put on those rope burns ought to make most of the irritation go away by tomorrow morning. I can give you something for the pain, but I'd prefer not to."

"Why?"

The doctor frowned. "There is some evidence being published in the medical journals that opiates complicate the problems of head injuries."

"Then how about a little whiskey?"

The doctor smiled. "I think that might be in order once we get you over to that cot."

He helped Clint up and over to the cot, then eased him into a sitting position saying, "A quick drink and then I want you to lie down flat."

"I'll do it."

The doctor went to a cabinet and produced a bottle and two glasses which he filled to the brim. Handing one to Clint, he raised his glass. "You're a very lucky man to be alive."

Clint tossed his liquor down neat. "I suspect I am."

The doctor smacked his lips. "Do you have any idea who might have shot you?"

"I do." Clint hesitated. "But Doc, I'd just as soon keep that to myself."

Dr. Tarver nodded. "It might be healthier for me if I didn't know anyway. Good night. I'll leave the bottle right here by your cot. But I'd advise you against overindulging with a concussion. It will most certainly compound any hangover."

"Thanks for the warning. And before you go, would you mind bringing my gun and holster over here."

"Are you in some danger?"

"It's possible, but unlikely," Clint said, thinking of Ben Towers. "I think that the man who shot me is probably miles away by now."

"Let's hope so."

Clint said nothing in response. "I've got to get after him as soon as I can, Doc. If I don't, he's the kind of man that will hide his trail and I might never pick it up again."

"I understand," the doctor said, "but if you try to do too much too soon, you might be endangering your health. As a physician, it's my duty to make that clear."

"And you have," Clint said, pouring himself another glass whiskey to ease the throb in his head. "So thanks."

After the doctor was gone, Clint checked his sixgun. He would try and sleep during the few hours that remained until dawn and he'd keep his gun at his side—just in case.

But sleep eluded the Gunsmith. He kept thinking about Lucy and her six-year-old daughter and wondering if he would ever find that little girl. Ben Towers was the key. He was the only man that could lead the Gunsmith to the little girl, and now Towers was probably putting distance between himself and Aquarius.

Clint became so frustrated that he forced himself to sit upright. He tried to stand but the dizziness returned and he quickly sat down again.

Frustrated, he cradled his head in his hands, and it was just about then that he heard the floor creak out in the hallway. Clint reached for his sixgun, thinking that his poor head might be playing tricks on him. But a moment later, he heard the floor protest again under the weight of a man.

Clint was sitting on a white sheet that covered the cot, and, with the turbanlike bandage around his head, he knew that he made an altogether too obvious target. He tore the bandage off, dropped to the floor, and scooted to an area of the room where the shadows were deepest.

The door opened and Clint held his breath. It was very dark, but he thought he could see the outline of a figure tiptoeing forward. There was a better than average chance that the figure belonged to the doctor and he was returning for something he might need or had forgotten, but the Gunsmith was not in the mood to take chances.

Cocking back the hammer of his gun, Clint shouted, "Freeze!"

His answer was a muzzle flash. Clint answered it with fire of his own. He unleashed three rounds. Over the loud gunfire he thought he heard a cry of pain, and then the dark silhouette vanished. Boots pounded in the doctor's hallway and a door slammed.

"Dammit!" the Gunsmith raged, coming to his feet. He took two faltering steps before the dizziness sent him blindly reeling into the examining table.

The Gunsmith was still cussing when a kerosene lamp blazed in the hallway and Dr. Tarver came rushing through the door to kneel beside him.

"Are you all right!"

"If I had a new head I'd be one hell of a lot better," Clint said, bitterly disappointed that he'd allowed Ben Towers to escape.

"Here," Tarver said, "let me help you back to your cot."

Clint almost fainted as the doctor got him back to the cot and a pillow under his head. "I let him get away," the Gunsmith whispered. "I let him get away!"

Dr. Tarver left his side for a moment but returned to hold a forefinger up before the Gunsmith's eyes. "He may have gotten away," the doctor said, "but he didn't do so entirely unscathed. And judging from the amount of blood that has stained my hallway to the back door, I'd say you hit your man rather solidly."

The Gunsmith closed his eyes and gripped the sides of his cot. "Good," he said, "but if someone comes looking for you to help take care of a gunshot, you'd better let me sit up and take another try."

"Who is it?"

Clint opened his eyes and looked up at the doctor. "His real name is Ben Towers. He's a professional gunfighter and hired killer. He came here posing as a mining engineer. He was in cahoots with your new assayer and banker. They were going to salt a mine with gold and sell stocks."

"And people would fall for that kind of thing?"

"If it's done well, they'll fall for it every time."

The doctor shook his head. "Well, at least it's over and the poor citizens of this town have you to thank."

Clint shook his head with dejection. "It isn't over until I find Ben Towers—alive or dead. And if he's dead, I might never find a little girl whose mother wants her very badly."

Tarver reached for the bottle and drank from it straight. "There's not much night left and neither of us are going to get any sleep. Why don't you tell me the whole story from start to finish."

"All right," Clint said after a long pause, "I might as well. Ben Towers is either dying, or he's leaving Aquarius as fast as a horse will carry him. Either way, I might have helped the people of your town, Doc, but until I find little Lisa, I've failed."

"You're a damned hard taskmaster for yourself."

Clint took the bottle from the doctor and treated himself to another drink. "It's a damned hard life," he said before he began his troubled story.

NINETEEN

When the Gunsmith prepared to ride out of Aquarius two days later, Dr. Tarver was almost livid with anger.

"You need a month or more to rest!" he snorted. "Two days isn't nearly long enough for a man in your condition!"

"Since Towers hasn't needed your services and since you're the only sawbones in Aquarius," Clint replied, "then I have to assume that he's not too badly wounded. That being the case, every hour that passes is another hour that he can put more distance between us. I have to go after him now, Doc. A professional killer like that will leave a real cold trail if you give him more than a day or two head start."

"Oh yeah, well what if you pitch off your horse and really break your neck this time?"

"That can't happen."

Doc Tarver bristled. "And why the hell not!"

"Because I'm riding a mule," Clint said, clapping the doctor on the shoulder and then passing out of his office on the way to the livery. He called back over his shoulder, "Quit worrying about me!"

"Someone sure as the hell better," the doctor complained.

Clint rode out of Aquarius less than an hour later. He wasn't sure exactly where he was going, but something told him that Ben Towers, wounded and now alone, might well head back toward Quartz, Arizona, where lawyer Mooney could give him money and a hiding place.

So the Gunsmith reined his mule southwest, and every man that he met on the trail he questioned because, hurt or healthy, Ben Towers was the kind of man that would be remembered.

In a little mining town called Rocky Ridge, Clint struck paydirt.

"Sure," an old man sitting in a rocking chair said, "I seen a man fitting that description come riding through just yesterday. He was on a dapple mare and you could tell that he wasn't feelin' so good because he was pale as chalk dust. He asked me if we had a doctor hereabouts and I said no, but there was one just on down the road in Prospect."

"How much farther?"

"Funny, that was his first question, too. Prospect is another eight miles on down this road. You can't miss it."

"Does this doctor have an office right on the main street?"

"He sure does. Doc Witherspoon has been practicing medicine as long as I can remember and that's more'n thirty years. You can't miss his place."

"Much obliged."

"Nice lookin' mule you got there. Some folks can't stand them, but it's been my experience they're smarter and more sure-footed than horses."

Clint patted his mule. "I like this one just fine."

"You want to sell him, you can get a good price hereabouts."

"No thanks," Clint said, reining the mule back onto the road and setting off at a steady, ground-eating trot.

It took him an hour to reach Prospect. It was nice town, bigger and more prosperous looking than most in these mountains. Dr. Witherspoon's office had a big sign hanging out in front.

Clint looked for a dapple mare and when he saw one, his heart began to pump faster. The horse was tied just two doors down from the doctor's office. When the Gunsmith pulled his mule up beside the animal, he saw dark, crusted blood on the saddle.

Clint dismounted, tipped back his Stetson, and leaned his forehead against his own saddle. Movement tended to made his head swim a little, and sometimes, like now, he broke into a cold sweat and felt queasy in the gut. Doc Tarver had warned him that he'd feel awful if he didn't stay flat on his back, but a man could do that when he'd finished the job he'd set out to do.

Clint waited almost a full minute. When he felt stronger, he pulled his hat brim down and walked a little unsteadily toward the doctor's office. He didn't expect that Towers would be there now, but the doctor would know where he was laid up.

"Good afternoon." Clint stepped into the office and saw a tall, gaunt old man in a white smock mixing medicines.

"Why, good afternoon!" The doctor looked at Clint's poor color and added, "Though I expect that it ain't so good for a man in your condition."

"I have seen better days," Clint admitted, a new bout of dizziness driving him toward a chair.

"Here now," the doctor said. "You ought to be in bed! Let me take a look at that head of yours."

Clint removed his hat. He'd insisted that he wouldn't wear a big bandage while on the trail, so Dr. Tarver had put a few stitches into his scalp and sent him on his way.

Dr. Witherspoon clucked his tongue and reached for some iodine. He asked a few questions and then he cleaned and rebandaged the bullet crease. "You're lucky to be alive, but from the looks of you, I'd say that you ought to be flat on your back in bed for a month or two."

"I can't just now," Clint said before he went into a careful description of Ben Towers.

"Sure, he's in town. Took a bullet in the side and lost a lot of blood. The bullet had passed right through his body so all I had to do was clean it up a mite."

"Where is he now?"

"He's staying with the widow Walker. I been meanin' to have a boy take his horse on down to the widow's corral."

"That would be the dapple mare outside."

"Yeah." The doctor's eyes narrowed. "Are you after the man or what?"

"I'm after him," Clint said. "He's a killer named Ben Towers and he's the one I can thank for this scalp wound."

"How do I know that *you're* not the killer?"

"You don't," Clint said. "But in my saddlebags I've got a few letters I keep from people like the Governor of Texas thanking me for being a lawman. On the other hand, if this town has a sheriff, you might just find a wanted poster on Ben Towers."

"Maybe I'll just mosey by the sheriff's office and have a look."

"Do that," Clint said. "In the meantime, do you have any smelling salts?"

"What for?"

"To clear my head in case I catch a dizzy spell about the same time that I meet up with Ben Towers again."

"You mean to kill him?"

"Arrest him."

"Then why don't you let our sheriff do it for you? It's his job and if there's a reward, he's going to want it anyway."

But the Gunsmith shook his head stubbornly. "No thanks. If there is a reward, I know some people who have suffered because of Towers and I'll see that they get it. Besides, I don't want any outside interference. I've been chasing this man a long, long time and I mean to do things my way."

The doctor's expression showed plainer than words that he wasn't very convinced, but he charged Clint a dollar and gave him smelling salts and directions to the widow Walker's house.

"She's a sharp-tongued, mean-faced woman," the doctor said as the Gunsmith climbed on his mule. "But she's got a little girl with blond hair and blue eyes that's the closest thing to an angel you'll ever see on this earth."

"How old?" Clint asked suddenly.

"Oh, six or so I'd guess."

"Thanks," Clint said. "Is her name Lisa?"

"Nope. It's Mary."

"I wouldn't bet on that," Clint said.

"Now what the hell is that supposed to mean?" the doctor demanded.

"It means her name is probably Lisa." Clint reached out and untied the dapple mare, then reined the mule off and continued down the street.

His head was spinning and his face was bathed in cold sweat but he felt more hopeful right that minute that he had in weeks, because all his instincts told him that he was finally about to find Madam Lucy's long-lost darling girl.

TWENTY

The doctor had given Clint a good description of the widow Walker's house, and it wasn't much to speak of. Just a shack with peeling paint, a picket fence with most of the pickets missing, and the remnants of a flower bed. Once, the house had probably been fixed up real cute, but that must have been a good many years ago.

Clint dismounted two houses up from the shack and tied the dapple mare. As for the mule, he just dropped the reins and hoped the animal would stick around.

"Can I help you?" an old lady called from her front porch.

"No, ma'am."

"Well you ain't goin' to leave that mule loose, now are you?"

"He'll stay out of trouble," Clint promised.

"Like hell he will!" the old woman cried, jumping out of her rocking chair. "Look, he's already going after my roses!"

Clint whirled around to see his mule going after the roses as if they were candy. He grabbed the mule's reins and pulled the animal away.

"Sorry about that, ma'am!" he called, forcing a smile. "He must have a little goat in him."

"Well you must have a little idiot in you for leavin' him untied."

"Yes, ma'am," Clint said.

"And don't you leave that horse there either! They crap and draw flies."

"Yes, ma'am," Clint said, untying the horse and remounting. He waved at the bitchy old woman and rode around her house and into the alley. He came up behind the widow Walker's house and found a small tree where he tied the dapple and turned the mule loose. "There's nothing here you can eat except weeds and tin cans, damn you, Rusty."

Clint studied the rear of the shack, which was a mess and filled with rusted tin cans and other trash. A few scrawny chickens were scratching around in a small pen, and the back door of the shack was hanging off kilter on broken hinges.

But what really attracted Clint's attention was the clothesline. For on it was a man's shirt as well as a child's pants and underclothes.

Clint hesitated beside the mule, not quite sure of what to do now. If he just grabbed the child, threw her on the dapple mare, and raced off, most likely everyone in town would think he was a damned kidnapper with evil intentions in his heart. There would be a posse and a chase. Clint knew that the mule wasn't fast enough to outrun pursuit, although the dapple mare looked fast and strong.

He was thinking about Ben Towers too. Most likely the man would be inside recovering from his bullet wound, and if he had the opportunity to grab the child and use her as a shield, he'd do it.

Clint expelled a deep breath. This was going to be a dicy proposition any way he cut it. And since he could not see an easy way around Ben Towers to the girl, he just started forward across the yard. Maybe Towers was taking a nap. In that case, Clint could pistol-whip the killer, tie him across his own saddle and explain to the little girl about her real mother.

The Gunsmith was thinking along these lines as he moved

silently across the backyard, stepping around the debris on his way to the broken back door. Suddenly, however, he heard the distinct sound of flesh striking flesh, and a little girl screamed.

Her scream was immediately followed by a woman's shrill voice, "I told you *never* to use my hair brush on that puppy! Never!"

This was followed by another sharp crack of flesh on flesh and it sent Clint charging through the back door. The inside of the shack was cluttered and filthy. Clint saw a woman with her hand upraised leaning over a child who was holding a puppy.

At the sight and sound of the Gunsmith, the woman whirled toward a doorway; that told Clint where he would find Ben Towers. The Gunsmith shot past the girl and widow Walker toward the door. He arrived to see Ben Towers raise a pistol and fire.

Clint jumped back. A bullet ate a big chunk of the door-jamb and a splinter tore a nasty gash in Clint's cheek. But his own gun was in his hand, and when he shoved it around the door he blindly fired three shots in Towers's direction, then pulled his arm back.

Widow Walker shrieked like a banshee and threw herself at Clint, clawing for his eyes. The Gunsmith managed to get his forearm up to protect his face, knocked the woman back, and stepped into the doorway.

Ben Towers was dying. One of the Gunsmith's bullets had found his chest and he was bent over at the waist, coughing blood.

Clint whirled around and the widow drove a knife at him. The Gunsmith ducked under the knife, which plunged into the wall. Clint managed to get his arms around the widow and propelled her into the bedroom, slamming the door shut behind him.

"You killed him!" the widow screamed, grabbing a chipped water pitcher and hurling it at the Gunsmith. "You killed my man!"

Clint ducked, and the water basin shattered against the wall. He looked back and saw that the little girl was hugging her puppy and sobbing quietly. Clint shut the door, not wanting her to see Ben Towers as he died.

"I'm taking the girl back to her real mother," he said, advancing toward the woman, who retreated with mounting fear. "I'm taking her back where she belongs."

"No you're not! She's mine!"

Clint cocked back the hammer of his sixgun and aimed it at the woman. "You don't deserve any child, especially one that isn't even your own flesh and blood. Are you ready to die?"

The shred of courage or anger that was holding Widow Walker erect broke, and she fell to her knees begging for her life.

"Don't kill me! Please don't kill me!" she cried in wretched terror.

"Gunsmith!" Towers whispered in a faint voice.

Clint forgot about the cowering woman. He went to the killer's side and studied the crimson stain on his chest. Towers was struggling to breathe, and his eyes were wet and filled with pain. Clint doubted that the man could even see him.

"What?"

"I'm . . . I'm glad a man like you killed me," Towers choked. "I always . . . always was afraid a nobody would backshoot me."

"I'm taking your daughter back to her real mother," Clint said. "I can forgive most anything but not what you allowed to happen to your daughter. How could you leave her here like this!"

The man's eyes blazed with anger. "You . . . you don't . . ."

Ben Towers's mouth worked frantically but no words came, and the man sighed deeply and lay still.

"See!" the woman screamed. "You killed him!"

"He needed killing," the Gunsmith said. "His saddled

dapple mare is tied out back with his bedroll, a good Winchester rifle, and a pair of saddlebags. I'm taking any money I find in them for the girl, but you can sell the horse, saddle and rifle. Ought to bring you more than a hundred dollars—if you keep your mouth shut. Otherwise, the sheriff will want to take everything and you'll likely never see a penny."

"Well what about him!" the widow cried. "What am I supposed to do about his body!"

"Tear up your floor and bury him. Or just wait until I'm gone and then say he shot himself to death." Clint waved his hand with distraction. "I don't give a damn what you do as long as that girl out there never hears from you again."

"He was her real father!" the widow cried. "You killed her *real* father."

"Well," Clint said, "if I did, then Ben Towers might have done one good thing in his life."

Clint left the woman, closing the door behind him. The little girl was gone!

He rushed outside and found her hiding under an old tarp, hugging her puppy. Her cheeks were wet with tears and her blue eyes were round with fright.

"Hi there," Clint said awkwardly. "I'm a friend of your mother and I've come to take you away."

The little girl shrank away in fear. She was clothed in a filthy dress, her blonde hair was tangled and unbrushed, she looked underfed, and she was puffy around the eyes where the widow Walker had slapped her.

Clint wanted to take the poor little waif in his arms and comfort her, but something told him that if he reached for the child, she would recoil in terror.

"Listen," Clint said, "your real mother loves you very much. She's given up everything trying to get you back. She sent me to find you."

The girl stared at him so intently he wondered if six years of mistreatment and beatings had addled her mind.

"What's her name, Mister?"

Clint grinned. "Your mother's name is Miss Lucy. And she's real pretty. She says your real name is Lisa."

The child cocked her head sideways and frowned. "Lisa? No, it's not—my name is Mary and this is Pepper."

Clint reached out very slowly and petted the puppy who licked his hand and wagged its tail energetically. "He's a nice puppy. I'm sure that he loves you very much. Just like your real mother. Shall we go see her now?"

The girl considered the proposition very, very carefully. Clint wasn't sure what he would have said if the girl had told him no. Fortunately, however, she nodded her head. "If we can take Pepper, I'll go."

"We'll take him all right," Clint said.

"And you won't hurt him? She said she'd hurt him if I didn't behave."

"She won't hurt you ever again," Clint vowed, glancing back at the shack. The widow Walker was standing just inside the busted door, peering through the crack at them.

"Let's go," Clint said, gently taking the girl's arm.

She clung fiercely to the puppy and Clint lifted them both. The girl was just skin and bone, and the puppy peed nervously on his shirtfront, but Clint didn't mind. He carried them both to the mule, sat them on his saddle, and mounted behind.

"Does my real mother live far, far away?"

"I'm afraid so."

The girl was silent for a moment as Clint picked up his reins, then she said, "Will we travel all night?"

"Probably ought to."

Lisa considered this in somber silence. Beside them, the dapple mare whinnied anxiously, but Clint didn't even look back as he reined the mule away. It was his full intention to put as much distance between Prospect and himself as was humanly possible during the next few days.

Before he returned to Quartz, Arizona, and delivered this child to her mother, Clint wanted to stop in Prescott and see how Rosie and Duke were getting along. He fervently hoped that Eli had nursed Duke back to soundness again. It wasn't that he didn't like this big mule—because he did— but there were times like now when a man wished for a faster conveyance.

As for Rosie, there was just no telling how she'd be thinking or acting now that she'd been introduced to the respectable bachelors of Prescott. Clint hoped that the girl had found herself a beau, one that would be hard-working and anxious for a good wife. One thing for sure, whoever married Rosie was going to have a handful of woman.

After Prescott, Clint would take the girl on down to Quartz and her waiting mother. That, he suspected, would be the diciest part of all. Miss Lucy would need to leave Quartz and start a new life for herself and her daughter. But first, there was James Mooney to settle a score with.

Clint expelled a deep breath. Just thinking about all the difficulties he still faced made his poor head throb and pound.

"Mister?"

He looked down at the girl. "Yes, Lisa?"

"I'm hungry."

Clint reached back into his saddlebags and rummaged around until he found a dried apple. He handed it to the girl feeling sure she would turn her freckled little nose up at the dried piece of fruit, but she didn't. In fact, she devoured the apple like it was a piece of candy.

"Anything else, Mister?"

He thought a minute. "I've got some raisins that I feed this mule."

"I *love* raisins! So does Pepper."

Clint scooped out a handful of raisins and gave them to the child. The mule, catching sight of his treats being devoured by the child and her puppy, brayed with dissatisfaction.

"Get along, you!" Clint snorted, pounding the beast with his heels.

The mule brayed again but Clint paid it no mind. In fact, he fed the hungry little girl and her puppy every damned raisin in his saddlebag just to spite the sorry mule and make it angry enough to hurry along toward Prescott.

TWENTY-ONE

Though it seemed like years since Clint had been through Prescott, it had only been a few hard months. Clint's first stop was at Eli's stable to see Duke.

"He's a beauty," Lisa whispered as Clint lifted her high up on the gelding's back. "A black beauty."

"He's a fine animal and a friend," Clint said, grinning from ear to ear because Duke was sound again. "I care for him the way you care for that puppy."

"Can we take him with us?"

"You bet," Clint said. "I've already sold Eli our mule and so we'll have a good meal on the town tonight and then we'll be on our way tomorrow morning."

Lisa nodded agreeably. In one of the mining towns that they had passed through, Clint had spent ten dollars buying the child a couple of pretty new dresses and a brush of her own. Like the widow woman that Lisa had lived with, Clint didn't much approve of the girl brushing her dog with her own hairbrush, but he chose not to make an issue of it.

"And there's someone else I want you to meet," Clint said, thinking of Rosie. "She's pretty too."

Lisa consented to leave her puppy with Eli and the Gunsmith proudly escorted the little girl over to Doctor Williams's fine house.

"Well Clint Adams!" the doctor exclaimed. "I was beginning to wonder if we'd ever see you back in Prescott."

Clint shook the man's hand warmly, then introduced him to Lisa, who was looking as pretty as a doll in her new dress with her face scrubbed and her hair brushed to a shine.

"We've come to see Rosie," the Gunsmith said.

The doctor's smile faded. "I'm afraid that you're a little late, Clint."

"What does that mean?"

"It means that she is engaged to be married to young Bob Tillison. Maybe you've heard of the Tillison Ranches?"

"Did you say 'ranches'?"

"Yes. The Tillisons are an old ranching family. They've made a lot of money and Bob—to my way of thinking— is the best of their kids. He's going to be a medical doctor, which doesn't make his father too happy with him— or me."

Clint was stunned. "I would imagine not. When are they leaving Prescott?"

"Actually," the doctor said, "they're going to be married in three days and leave for the East Coast a week later."

"I couldn't be happier for Rosie," Clint said, meaning it.

"Her name is now Rosalinda," the doctor said with a wink. "And I couldn't be happier either. When you brought her on that travois . . . well, she was not only hurt but a little rough around the edges, if you know what I mean."

"Sure. I know."

"So I introduced her around a little to some of the women I thought would make a good example for her and they did."

The old doctor shook his head and chuckled. "You should see Rosalinda now, Clint! She looks as if she's spent her entire life in a finishing school. The transformation is purely remarkable. She just bowled poor old Bob right off his feet. It was a whirlwind courtship."

"Can I still meet your pretty friend?" Lisa chirped.

"We'll see," Clint told her. He looked back to the doctor. "Just tell Rosie that I asked about her and wished her all the happiness in the world with her new husband and life."

"I will," the doctor promised.

Clint had difficulty hiding his disappointment that evening. He hadn't realized how much he'd been counting on seeing Rosie again. But he supposed that not seeing her again was best, at least for her.

So the Gunsmith put on his best face and soon forgot his disappointment as he treated Lisa to a big dinner at the best steak house in Prescott. And that night, he and Lisa trudged back to the Eli's livery where he spread his bedroll out for himself on the straw. Nearbye, Lisa and Pepper—puppy and child—fell into the dreamless sleep of the very young and innocent.

The Gunsmith was tired himself, and, though anything but innocent, he was soon sleeping peacefully. But sometime in the middle of the night, he was roused into wakefulness by a showering of kisses.

"What . . ."

"It's me, darling!" Rosie whispered happily. "Doc told me you got back this afternoon and as soon as the way was clear, I hurried on over to see you."

Clint sat up and knuckled the sleep from his eyes. It was pretty dark in the barn, but there was enough moonlight flooding through the opening in the loft to see that Rosie was aglow and prettier than a picture poster girl.

"I love you," she told him, taking his hands. "Is that Miss Lucy's little girl?"

"Yes. It took awhile, but I found her."

Rosie pulled away for a moment and rolled across the hay to study the child and her sleeping puppy. Clint heard a catch in her throat when she said, "I want a girl just like this one of my own someday, Clint. I want bunches of them!"

"You'll have them then," Clint said.

Rosie bent and kissed Lisa's cheek, then scooted across the hay and back to Clint's side. She took his hands again and said, "I'd like to make love with you right now more than I've ever wanted anyone in my life but . . ."

"But you can't," Clint said gently. "Because you love Bob and are engaged to marry him."

Rosie nodded her head. "But I love you too!"

"I know, but now that you're engaged to be married, everything is different. You can't be one man's wife and make love to another man."

"But I'm not married yet."

"I know," Clint said, finding it hard to believe what he was saying, because the sight, smell and touch of this girl was stirring his passions. "But when you agree to marry someone for love, you've made a pledge to each other. And it's one that I know you really want to keep."

She gulped and dipped her chin up and down in reluctant agreement. "I wish I didn't love you too," she confessed. "I feel guilty enough about just coming here but I couldn't stand the thought of never seeing you again."

Rosie was quiet for a minute, then blurted, "I will see you again, won't I?"

"I can't say," he told her. "But it's likely. The most important thing is that you are happy and in love. Everything else comes second."

"You never will," she said. "I don't care if I'm married one hundred years and die of happiness in Bob's arms. I'll always remember you, and sometimes dream about how we made love."

Clint was beginning to lose his resolve and high purpose. "You better get out of here right now."

Rosie nodded and sniffled. She kissed him one last time, long and passionately and just as Clint was reaching to pull her down on the straw and say to hell with honor, Rosie squirted out of his arms and vanished.

The Gunsmith expelled a deep breath and eased back down on his bedroll. If it had not been for the girl entrusted in his care, he would have searched out a dance hall girl or even a lady of the night for a little relief. But Lisa's welfare came way ahead of his own desires, so Clint closed his eyes.

For a good long while he could taste Rosie's sweet kiss and smell her body.

"Life is hard, ain't it hard," he muttered before falling asleep.

In the morning, he awoke to see shafts of dusty light filtering down through the cracks in the roof and walls. Lisa and the puppy were playing quietly together, wrestling and giggling.

"Are you ready to go now?" Lisa asked.

"I guess I am," Clint said, pushing the thought of Rosie from his mind.

He would buy them both a big breakfast and they'd saddle Duke and gallop off to Quartz. But sure as the sun was up and this Arizona day was warming nicely, he was going to miss Rosie and his fine mule.

TWENTY-TWO

It was dark when Clint and Lisa rode into Quartz. The Ace High Saloon was going full blast and Lucy's Place was as busy as could be with men streaming in and out after being with the girls. Clint didn't quite know how to handle things from this point on. He was sure that Lucy Mullane wouldn't want her daughter to know she was a madam, keeper of the most famous brothel in Arizona.

"Where are we going?" the little girl asked, her eyes opened wide at the sight of so many revelers.

"I think we'll find ourselves a nice hotel room, darlin', and something for you and that dog to eat."

"He's not a dog! Pepper is a *puppy*!"

"Oh, I'm sorry," Clint said, "I keep forgetting."

In truth, he had fallen in love with the little girl but couldn't tolerate her damned puppy which kept pissing on them both, especially when he tried to push Duke into a trot or gallop. Both he and the girl reeked with urine, and the Gunsmith was ready to feed Pepper to the coyotes.

Clint found a hostelry at the north end of town. A quiet little place run by a hardworking family named Crampton, where for an extra two-bits you could take your meals.

"What a pretty daughter you have!" Mrs. Crampton exclaimed. "I should imagine you are very proud."

"I wish she was my daughter," Clint said. "Would you

157

mind watching over her for a little while? I need to do a few errands."

"Of course not!" Mrs. Crampton's nose twitched. "Perhaps we can even give her a bath and wash that putrid dress."

"Be obliged," Clint said, wishing he had the time to do the same thing. "And make sure that that puppy doesn't come to any harm. Lisa sets a big store to it."

"I understand."

Lisa was apprehensive about Clint leaving but after assuring her that she was not being deserted, he extracted himself and headed directly for Lucy's Place.

He was walking up the street when James Mooney exited the whorehouse. The cutthroat attorney was flanked by two gunmen. All three climbed into a fancy carriage and the driver whipped the team of horses and headed east out of town, no doubt to Mooney's big ranch. Clint instinctively ducked his head and pulled his hat low. He had to talk to Lucy before he and Mooney locked horns.

When Clint entered the brothel, its downstairs was packed and the fancy bar along the west wall was two deep with customers.

Clint headed for Lucy's upstairs room. But at the head of the stairs, his progress was blocked by a big man with arms like a blacksmith.

"Turn around, Mister," the guard rumbled. "No men are allowed up these stairs unless they're with one of the girls."

The guard was huge and ferocious looking. He stood well over six foot and would weigh at least 250 pounds, all of it muscle.

"I need to see Miss Lucy," Clint said. "It's business."

The giant shook his head. "She ain't here no more. Miss Annabelle runs things for Mr. Mooney now. And Miss Annabelle is with a customer."

"Where did Miss Lucy go?"

"I don't know and I don't care." At that moment, a man

and a woman came bumping off the second floor landing. The whore was painted up and a well-dressed man on her arm was pretty drunk and had to be eased down the stairs so he didn't fall and break his neck.

"Hi, honey," Annabelle said, giving a playful tug at Clint's crotch as she slipped past on her way down.

"Annabelle, remember me?" he called, hurrying after her. "We had a little fun about two months ago when I walked my horse in. Remember he was lame?"

"Honey," she said, "I always remember the handsome faces. What you want, a little pleasuring?"

"I got to talk to you privately," Clint said, grabbing Annabelle and pulling her away from the drunken man who was trying to buy her a drink.

"Listen, honey," Annabelle said, "I got regular customers to take care of. Now if you want to talk, don't come here on Saturday night. You understand?"

Annabelle was jerked roughly out of Clint's grasp by the man she'd been with, who slurred, "This lady is with me tonight. Find yourself another whore, Mister!"

Clint's fist traveled only six inches before exploding against the man's jaw. Clint caught the unconscious fellow and plunked him down in a chair, then pulled Annabelle aside again.

She wasn't happy. "Now what did you do that for! He's one of Mr. Mooney's best clients and I'm supposed to take care of him tonight!"

"Listen, dammit! I got to find Miss Lucy. I have her missing daughter!"

Annabelle's eyes widened. "You found Lisa!"

"Yes! And I thought Miss Lucy would be here to take her. But . . ."

Annabelle pulled the Gunsmith over to a table where they could talk privately. "Oh, my heavens!" she groaned. "What did you have to do, kill Ben Towers?"

"As a matter of fact, that's exactly what I had to do," Clint said.

"Does Mr. Mooney know you're in town yet?"

"No, but I'm sure the word will get around by tomorrow. So where is Lucy Mullane?"

"She quit and opened a cafe."

"What?"

Annabelle shrugged. "She kept saying that, when you returned with Lisa, she *had* to have a respectable line of work. Of course, no one but her believed that you'd come back. And where's Rosie?"

Clint started to tell the woman but changed his mind. Rosie had gone respectable too, and it was better if her name and whereabouts remained unknown in this town.

"Rosie is gone," Clint said, looking down at his hands and sighing deeply.

"Oh my heavens!" Annabelle cried. "The poor thing!"

Annabelle sniffled. "Everyone loved Rosie. Even me. She was so sweet and much too young to die."

Clint nodded his head. "Now tell me where I can find Miss Lucy so that I can deliver her daughter."

"She'll go crazy with joy," Annabelle said. "I wish I could be there to see them come together after all these years. Is the little girl real pretty?"

"Like an angel," Clint said. "She looks like her mother must have looked when she was a child. "So where is Lucy?" Clint asked again.

"She lives alone in a little house at the other end of town," Annabelle said, and then she proceeded to give Clint the directions.

After retrieving Lisa and her damned puppy, Clint had no trouble at all finding Lucy Mullane's house. When he knocked at her door, he saw a shadow pass before the curtain and then Lucy called out, "Who is it?"

"It's the Gunsmith, open up."

The door flew open and Lucy hardly glanced at Clint's face, as her eyes dropped down to see her daughter.

"Miss Lucy, meet your daughter and her puppy named Pepper," Clint said, feeling a painful lump in his throat build as tears of happiness began to roll down Lucy's cheeks.

Lucy dropped to her knees. Lisa stared at her mother, half scared, half excited. The puppy began to whimper. Then Lucy cried out with joy, swept them both into her arms, and hugged them with all her might as she began to sob.

Clint had to turn away. Few things in his life had moved him as deeply as this reunion, and if he could somehow find a way to settle the score with James Mooney so that the man could never again hurt either one of these two, then everything was going to be just fine in Quartz.

"I guess maybe I'll see you tomorrow," Clint said after a few awkward moments.

"Wait, please!" Lucy cried.

Clint had been about to step off the rickety front porch when Lucy touched his arm. "Thank you," she whispered.

"You're welcome." Clint cleared his throat. "Miss Lucy, I don't know what Mooney will do when he finds out about this, but he's the kind of man that will want to get even with me. I think it'd be best if I didn't see you or Lisa until the dust settles. Do you understand what I'm saying?"

"Of course. But what . . ."

"The only thing you can do is say a little prayer that it all works out for the best."

Lisa dropped her puppy and came to stand before Clint. "Where are you going?"

"Not far," he told her. "I just have to do a few things. I'll be back before too long. You be a good girl and stay with your mother."

Lisa nodded but she looked ready to cry. "But I don't want you to go away!"

"I have to," he said. "But I will be back. I promise."

When the little girl nodded with reluctant acceptance, Clint turned and strode away but it was hard. He moved back down the street to his horse, staying in the shadows, and, as he walked, he made his plans. He wouldn't wait until Mooney came hunting for him. Instead, he would go right after the man and catch him by surprise.

Clint untied Duke and shoved his boot into his stirrup. He remembered hearing about Mooney's big ranch and house about five mile east of town. Maybe it was crazy to go where Mooney had all the advantages, but Clint had been thinking about the ruthless lawyer for a long time, and he was impatient for a showdown.

A showdown that couldn't wait a single hour longer.

TWENTY-THREE

Although the hour grew late, Clint had no difficulty following Mooney's carriage tracks out to his Rocking M Ranch. When the Gunsmith arrived at the main gate, he opened it and left it swinging in the night breeze. About a mile up ahead, he could see the dark outline of big trees and a roof line against the night sky. A little lower down, he saw tiny squares of light in what he judged to be upstairs windows.

The Gunsmith stood up in his stirrups and stretched, massaging the small of his back. He'd been on horseback too much during the past few weeks, and he was stiff and weary. But now that he had made his decision to confront James Mooney, there was little point in procrastinating. His best move would be to sneak into the house, arrest his man in connection with the mine swindle, and whisk him off to the territorial court system before anyone realized that he was missing.

It was a tall order and Clint had no illusions. If he were discovered tonight, he would be overwhelmed and killed. To make matters even worse, there was no telling what Mooney might do to Lucy and her daughter in reprisal. If it hadn't been for the latter fact, Clint might have just ridden on by the ranch and put this entire mess behind him.

Instead, the Gunsmith angled to the south, riding through bunches of cattle in the pale moonlight while the mournful howl of a pack of coyotes sounded somewhere off in the distant hills. It took Clint nearly an hour to circle the ranch house and outbuildings, and he tied Duke behind what appeared to be a large blacksmith shop.

The Gunsmith pulled the brim of his Stetson even lower on his forehead. He checked his sixgun. When he was satisfied that he was as ready as he would ever be, Clint moved directly across the ranch yard toward the house.

When he was right in the middle of the yard, the same pair that Clint had seen escorting Mooney out of Lucy's Place emerged. They were laughing and in good spirits, and Clint figured that Mooney had treated them to whores and some of his own whiskey. That would more than account for their laughter.

The Gunsmith turned and began to saunter off toward a horse corral, and the pair paid him no attention. When Clint heard the bunkhouse door slam, he reversed direction back toward the ranch house. The downstairs was dark but lights blazed from a second story window that Clint figured had to be Mooney's bedroom.

Would there be a guard posted on the first floor? Clint very much doubted it, because Mooney would never expect an enemy to come onto his ranch where he was most closely protected. But just to be sure, the Gunsmith peeked in one of the front windows. He couldn't see anything.

Taking one last glance over his shoulder, Clint stepped up to the front door, turned the knob, and passed into the entryway. He closed the door softly and remained motionless, his eyes adjusting to the darkness. He could hear someone tromping around upstairs. The Gunsmith groped his way down the hall to the staircase and slowly began to climb.

He was almost at the top of the stairs when one stair squeaked loudly. Clint froze, hand on gunbutt.

"Who is it! Mace? George?"

Clint took the last two stairs in a rush and caught James Mooney standing barefoot and bare-chested, wearing only his pants. "What the . . . who the hell are you?"

Clint stood rooted in the dark hallway. "It's me, Clint Adams. The man they call the Gunsmith. Remember?" Clint asked, cocking back the hammer of his gun.

Mooney's jaw dropped. He couldn't see the sixgun, but now he knew it was in Clint's hand and no doubt aimed at his chest.

"What the hell do you want!"

"We got a date with a federal judge. I'm going to see that you spend a long, long time in prison for your conspiracy with Ben Towers and his friends. I'll just bet there are even papers in your safe or hidden somewhere in this house that will tie you into salting those gold mines. Tie you in tighter than ticks on a hound."

"You're bluffing! You don't have anything on me! And I'm a lawyer. Do you really think that I'd be stupid enough to keep evidence against myself where it could be found?"

Mooney grinned, then snickered. "Maybe what you really want is a job. Maybe you'd like to clean spitoons in my saloon or empty the chamber pots in my whorehouse."

When Clint said nothing, Mooney added, "Or maybe you just want a few dollars and your life. I might be willing to give you both."

"I'm taking you in for a trial, with or without written evidence. You see," Clint said, "Ben Towers is willing to testify that you were behind the whole swindle. He's doesn't want to take all the blame. He says the mine-salting idea was yours alone."

"You're lying!" Mooney hissed. "I'll bet you killed him!"

"Then let's go find out," Clint said, motioning the man forward with his gun.

Mooney took a half step forward, then lunged at the door. He was extremely quick and managed to slam it shut, but before he could throw the bolt Clint drove his shoulder into the door and knocked it flying. He and Mooney both crashed to the floor.

Mooney knocked Clint's gun aside and threw himself on

the Gunsmith. They rolled, punching, gouging and clawing. Mooney was surprisingly strong. What he lacked in experience, he more than made up for in savagery. He drove his thumbs up into Clint's face, searching for his eyesockets.

Clint turned his face away protectively, butted the man with his forehead, then butted him again. Mooney cried out in pain and rolled hard to the left, throwing Clint aside, then leapt to his feet and started to open his window and yell for help.

But Clint grabbed him around the neck in a choke hold and wrestled him backward. Mooney made a strangling sound and hammered the Gunsmith with his elbows until Clint was forced to break his hold. They tumbled into a bureau, knocking over a kerosene lamp. The lamp crashed on the floor beside the window and the curtains went up in flames.

A cry was torn from Mooney's throat. With desperate rage, he threw himself at the Gunsmith. Heaving and grunting, they reeled around in circles and toppled across the bed, grunting, cursing and hammering each other with their fists.

Clint's head suddenly felt as if it were going to burst like an overripe melon. He felt dizzy and suddenly very weak. The lawyer rolled onto his chest and began to beat his face with both fists. Desperate and on the edge of losing consciousness, the Gunsmith kicked up his heels, wrapped them around Mooney's neck and jerked the man over backward. Dimly, he could hear the roar of the flames and feel the heat of the fire.

Mooney was beyond desperation. He jumped up toward his coat hanging on his bedpost and yanked a two-shot derringer from one of his pockets. Before he could raise the derringer, Clint grabbed Mooney's wrist, and they struggled for control of the weapon until the derringer exploded between their bodies with a muffled roar. Clint felt powder burn his chest and then the little pistol bucked again. Mooney suddenly went stiff against the Gunsmith. A split-second later, he shivered and collapsed dead on the floor.

Clint spun toward the window. The entire side of the wall was on fire and flames were driving up and overhead. The window shattered from the heat, and Clint knew that the house was going to go up like a box of tinder.

He scooped up his sixgun and raced back downstairs to see men running across the yard from the bunkhouse. Clint reversed direction and sprinted down the hall. It was so dark he collided with a back door. He found the doorknob and bulled his way outside, tripping over something and pitching head first into a post of some kind.

Dazed, dizzy and tasting blood, Clint climbed to his feet and unsteadily made his way around behind the blacksmith's shop.

Duke was stamping his hooves nervously and rolling his eyes because the ranch house had ignited like a torch. "Easy," Clint said, watching men dance around in front of the inferno in helpless confusion.

The Gunsmith removed his hat and dunked his head in a horse's watering trough. The shock of cold water instantly cleared his mind. He wiped his face dry with his sleeve, then untied Duke and hauled himself into the saddle.

For almost a full minute, the Gunsmith watched the flames licking up into the dark sky. Then he reined Duke away and rode silently off into the night. He would say a last goodbye to Lucy and to little Lisa and tell them that they no longer had anything to fear.

And then, he would leave this part of Arizona before his luck turned sour again.

Watch for

GHOST TOWN

127th novel in the exciting GUNSMITH series
from Jove

Coming in July!

SPECIAL PREVIEW!

Introducing a magnificent new series as big and bold as the American frontier . . .

THE HORSEMEN

The Ballous were the finest horsemen in the South, a Tennessee family famous for the training and breeding of glorious Thoroughbreds. When the Civil War devastated their home and their lives, they headed West—into the heart of Indian territory. As horsemen, they triumphed. As a family, they endured. But as pioneers in a new land, they faced unimaginable hardship, danger, and ruthless enemies. . . .

Turn the page for a preview of this exciting new western series . . .

The Horsemen

Now available from Diamond Books!

November 24, 1863—Just east of Chattanooga, Tennessee

The chestnut stallion's head snapped up very suddenly. Its nostrils quivered, then flared, testing the wind, tasting the approach of unseen danger. Old Justin Ballou's watchful eye caught the stallion's motion and he also froze, senses focused. For several long moments, man and stallion remained motionless, and then Justin Ballou opened the gate to the paddock and limped toward the tall Thoroughbred. He reached up and his huge, blue-veined hand stroked the stallion's muzzle. "What is it, High Man?" he asked softly. "What now, my friend?"

In answer, the chestnut dipped its head several times and stamped its feet with increasing nervousness. Justin began to speak soothingly to the stallion, his deep, resonant voice flowing like a mystical incantation. Almost at once, the stallion grew calm. After a few minutes, Justin said, as if to an old and very dear friend, "Is it one of General Grant's Union patrols this time, High Man? Have they come to take what little I have left? If so, I will gladly fight them to the death."

The stallion shook its head, rolled its eyes, and snorted as if it could smell Yankee blood. Justin's thick fingers scratched a special place behind the stallion's ear. The chestnut lowered its head to nuzzle the man's chest.

"Don't worry. It's probably another Confederate patrol,"

173

Justin said thoughtfully. "But what can they want this time?
I have already given them three fine sons and most of your
offspring. There is so little left to give—but they know that!
Surely they can see my empty stalls and paddocks."

Justin turned toward the road leading past his neat,
whitewashed fences that sectioned and cross-sectioned his
famous Tennessee horse ranch, known throughout the South
as Wildwood Farm. The paddocks were empty and silent.
This cold autumn day, there were proud mares with their
colts, and prancing fillies blessed the old man's vision and
gave him the joy he'd known for so many years. It was
the war—this damned killing Civil War. "No more!" Justin
cried. "You'll have no more of my fine horses or sons!"

The stallion spun and galloped away. High Man was
seventeen years old, long past his prime, but he and a
few other Ballou-bred stallions still sired the fastest and
handsomest horses in the South. Just watching the chestnut
run made Justin feel a little better. High Man was a living
testimony to the extraordinarily fine care he'd received all
these years at Wildwood Farms. No one could believe that
at his ripe age he could still run and kick his heels up like
a three-year-old colt.

The stallion ran with such fluid grace that he seemed to
float across the earth. When the Thoroughbred reached the
far end of the paddock, it skidded to a sliding stop, chest
banging hard against the fence. It spun around, snorted, and
shook its head for an expected shout of approval.

But not this day. Instead, Justin made himself leave the
paddock, chin up, stride halting but resolute. He could hear
thunder growing louder. Could it be the sound of cannon
from as far away as the heights that General Bragg and his
Rebel army now held in wait of the Union army's expected
assault? No, the distance was too great even to carry the roar
of heavy artillery. That told Justin that his initial hunch was
correct and the sound growing in his ears had to be racing
hoofbeats.

But were they enemy or friend? Blue coat or gray? Justin

planted his big work boots solidly in the dust of the country road; either way, he would meet them.

"Father!"

He recognized his fourteen-year-old daughter's voice and ignored it, wanting Dixie to stay inside their mansion. Justin drew a pepperbox pistol from his waistband. If this actually was a dreaded Union cavalry patrol, then someone was going to die this afternoon. A man could only be pushed so far and then he had to fight.

"Father!" Dixie's voice was louder now, more strident. "Father!"

Justin reluctantly twisted about to see his daughter and her oldest brother, Houston, running toward him. Both had guns clenched in their fists.

"Who is it!" Houston gasped, reaching Justin first and trying to catch his wind.

Justin did not dignify the stupid question with an answer. In a very few minutes, they would know. "Dixie, go back to the house."

"Please, I . . . I just can't!"

"Dixie! Do as Father says," Houston stormed. "This is no time for arguing. Go to the house!"

Dixie's black eyes sparked. She stood her ground. Houston was twenty-one and a man full grown, but he was still just her big brother. "I'm staying."

Houston's face darkened with anger and his knuckles whitened as he clutched the gun in his fist. "Dammit, you heard . . ."

"Quiet, the both of you!" Justin commanded. "Here they come."

A moment later a dust-shrouded patrol lifted from the earth to come galloping up the road.

"It's *our* boys," Dixie yelped with relief. "It's a Reb patrol!"

"Yeah," Houston said, taking an involuntary step forward, "but they been shot up all to hell!"

Justin slipped his gun back into his waistband and was

seized by a flash of dizziness. Dixie moved close, steadying him until the spell passed a moment later. "You all right?"

Justin nodded. He did not know what was causing the dizziness, but the spells seemed to come often these days. No doubt, it was the war. This damned war that the South was steadily losing. And the death of two of his five strapping sons and . . .

Houston had stepped out in front and now he turned to shout, "Mason is riding with them!"

Justin's legs became solid and strong again. Mason was the middle son, the short, serious one that wanted to go into medicine and who read volumes of poetry despite the teasing from his brothers.

Dixie slipped her gun into the pocket of the loose-fitting pants she insisted on wearing around the horses. She glanced up at her father and said, "Mason will be hungry and so will the others. They'll need food and bandaging."

"They'll have both," Justin declared without hesitation, "but no more of my Thoroughbreds!"

"No more," Dixie vowed. "Mason will understand."

"Yeah," Houston said, coming back to stand by his father, "but the trouble is, he isn't in charge. That's a captain he's riding alongside."

Justin was about to speak, but from the corner of his eyes, saw a movement. He twisted, hand instinctively lifting the pepperbox because these woods were crawling with both Union and Confederate deserters, men often half-crazy with fear and hunger.

"Pa, don't you dare shoot me!" Rufus "Ruff" Ballou called, trying to force a smile as he moved forward, long and loose limbed with his rifle swinging at his side.

"Ruff, what the hell you doing hiding in those trees!" Houston demanded, for he too had been startled enough to raise his gun.

If Ruff noticed the heat in his older brother's voice, he chose to ignore it.

"Hell, Houston, I was just hanging back a little to make

sure these were friendly visitors."

"It's Mason," Justin said, turning back to the patrol. "And from the looks of these boys, things are going from bad to worse."

There were just six men in the patrol, two officers and four enlisted. One of the enlisted was bent over nearly double with pain, a blossom of red spreading across his left shoulder. Two others were riding double on a runty sorrel.

"That sorrel is gonna drop if it don't get feed and rest," Ruff observed, his voice hardening with disapproval.

"All of their mounts look like they've been chased to hell and back without being fed or watered," Justin stated. "We'll make sure they're watered and grained before these boys leave."

The Ballous nodded. It never occurred to any of them that a horse should ever leave their farm in worse shape then when it had arrived. The welfare of livestock just naturally came first—even over their own physical needs.

Justin stepped forward and raised his hand in greeting. Deciding that none of the horses were in desperate circumstances, he fixed his attention on Mason. He was shocked. Mason was a big man, like his father and brothers, but now he appeared withered—all ridges and angles. His cap was missing and his black hair was wild and unkept. His cheeks were hollow, and the sleeve of his right arm had been cut away, and now his arm was wrapped in a dirty bandage. The loose, sloppy way he sat his horse told Justin more eloquently than words how weak and weary Mason had become after just eight months of fighting the armies of the North.

The patrol slowed to a trot, then a walk, and Justin saw the captain turn to speak to Mason. Justin couldn't hear the words, but he could see by the senior officer's expression that the man was angry and upset. Mason rode trancelike, eyes fixed on his family, lips a thin, hard slash instead of the expected smile of greeting.

Mason drew his horse to a standstill before his father and brothers. Up close, his appearance was even more shocking.

"Mason?" Justin whispered when his son said nothing. "Mason, are you all right?"

Mason blinked. Shook himself. "Father. Houston. Ruff. Dixie. You're all looking well. How are the horses?"

"What we got left are fine," Justin said cautiously. "Only a few on the place even fit to run. Sold all the fillies and colts last fall. But you knew that."

"You did the right thing to keep Houston and Ruff out of this," Mason said.

Houston and Ruff took a sudden interest in the dirt under their feet. The two youngest Ballou brothers had desperately wanted to join the Confederate army, but Justin had demanded that they remain at Wildwood Farm, where they could help carry on the family business of raising Thoroughbreds. Only now, instead of racetracks and cheering bettors, the Ballou horses swiftly carried messages between the generals of the Confederate armies. Many times the delivery of a vital message depended on horses with pure blazing speed.

"Lieutenant," the captain said, clearing his throat loudly, "I think this chatter has gone on quite long enough. Introduce me."

Mason flushed with humiliation. "Father, allow me to introduce Captain Denton."

Justin had already sized up the captain, and what he saw did not please him. Denton was a lean, straight-backed man. He rode as if he had a rod up his ass and he looked like a mannequin glued to the saddle. He was an insult to the fine tradition of Southern cavalry officers.

"Captain," Justin said without warmth, "if you'll order your patrol to dismount, we'll take care of your wounded and these horses."

"Private Wilson can't ride any father," Denton said. "And there isn't time for rest."

"But you *have* to," Justin argued. "These horses are—"

"Finished," Denton said. "We must have replacements; that's why we are here, Mr. Ballou."

Justin paled ever so slightly. "Hate to tell you this, Captain, but I'm afraid you're going to be disappointed. I've already given all the horses I can to the Confederacy—sons, too."

Denton wasn't listening. His eyes swept across the paddock.

"What about *that* one," he said, pointing toward High Man. "He looks to be in fine condition."

"He's past his racing prime," Houston argued. "He's our foundation sire now and is used strictly for breeding."

"Strictly for breeding?" Denton said cryptically. "Mr. Ballou, there is not a male creature on this earth who would not like to—"

"Watch your tongue, sir!" Justin stormed. "My daughter's honor will not be compromised!"

Captain Denton's eyes jerked sideways to Dixie and he blushed. Obviously, he had not realized Dixie was a girl with her baggy pants and a felt slouch hat pulled down close to her eyebrows. And a Navy Colt hanging from her fist.

"My sincere apologies." The captain dismissed her and his eyes came to rest on the barns. "You've got horses in those stalls?"

"Yes, but—"

"I'd like to see them," Denton said, spurring his own flagging mount forward.

Ruff grabbed his bit. "Hold up there, Captain, you haven't been invited."

"And since when does an officer of the Confederacy need to beg permission for horses so that *your* countrymen, as well as mine, can live according to our own laws!"

"*I'm* the law on this place," Justin thundered. "And my mares are in foal. They're not going to war, Captain. Neither they nor the last of my stallions are going to be chopped to pieces on some battlefield or have their legs ruined while trying to pull supply wagons. These are *Thoroughbred* horses, sir! Horses bred to race."

"The race," Denton said through clenched teeth, "is to see if we can bring relief to our men who are, this very moment, fighting and dying at Lookout Mountain and Missionary Ridge."

Denton's voice shook with passion. "The plundering armies of General Ulysses Grant, General George Thomas, and his Army of the Cumberland are attacking our soldiers right now, and God help me if I've ever seen such slaughter! Our boys are dying, Mr. Ballou! Dying for the right to determine the South's great destiny. We—not you and your piddling horses—are making the ultimate sacrifices! But maybe your attitude has a lot to do with why you married a Cherokee Indian woman."

Something snapped behind Justin Ballou's obsidian eyes. He saw the faces of his two oldest sons, one reported to have been blown to pieces by a Union battery in the battle of Bull Run and the other trampled to death in a bloody charge at Shiloh. Their proud mother's Cherokee blood had made them the first in battle and the first in death.

Justin lunged, liver-spotted hands reaching upward. Too late Captain Denton saw murder in the old man's eyes. He tried to rein his horse off, but Justin's fingers clamped on his coat and his belt. With a tremendous heave, Denton was torn from his saddle and hurled to the ground. Justin growled like a huge dog as his fingers crushed the breath out of Denton's life.

He would have broken the Confederate captain's neck if his sons had not broken his stranglehold. Two of the mounted soldiers reached for their pistols, but Ruff's own rifle made them freeze and then slowly raise their hands.

"Pa!" Mason shouted, pulling Justin off the nearly unconscious officer. "Pa, stop it!"

As suddenly as it had flared, Justin's anger ended, and he had to be helped to his feet. He glared down at the wheezing cavalry officer and his voice trembled when he said, "Captain Denton, I don't know how the hell you managed to get a commission in Jeff Davis's army, but I do know this: lecture me about sacrifice for the South again and I will break your fool neck! Do you hear me!"

The captain's eyes mirrored raw animal fear. "Lieutenant Ballou," he choked at Mason, "I *order* you in the name of the Army of the Confederacy to confiscate fresh horses!"

"Go to hell."

"I'll have you court-martialed and shot for insubordination!"

Houston drew his pistol and aimed it at Denton's forehead. "Maybe you'd better change your tune, Captain."

"No!"

Justin surprised them all by coming to Denton's defense. "If you shoot him—no matter how much he deserves to be shot—our family will be judged traitors."

"But . . ."

"Put the gun away," Justin ordered wearily. "I'll give him fresh horses."

"Pa!" Ruff cried. "What are you going to give to him? Our mares?"

"Yes, but not all of them. Just the youngest and the strongest. And those matched three-year-old stallions you and Houston are training."

"But, Pa," Ruff protested, "they're just green broke."

"I know, but this will season them in a hurry," Justin said levelly. "Besides, there's no choice. High Man leaves Wildwood Farm over my dead body."

"Yes, sir," Ruff said, knowing his father was not running a bluff.

Dixie turned away in anger and started toward the house. "I'll see we get food cooking for the soldiers and some fresh bandages for Private Wilson."

A moment later, Ruff stepped over beside the wounded soldier. "Here, let me give you a hand down. We'll go up to the house and take a look at that shoulder."

Wilson tried to show his appreciation as both Ruff and

Houston helped him to dismount. "Much obliged," he whispered. "Sorry to be of trouble."

Mason looked to his father. "Sir, I'll take responsibility for your horses."

"How can you do that?" Houston demanded of his brother. "These three-year-old stallions and our mares will go crazy amid all that cannon and rifle fire. No one but us can control them. It would be—"

"Then you and Ruff need to come on back with us," Mason said.

"No!" Justin raged. "I paid for their replacements! I've got the papers saying that they can't be drafted or taken into the Confederate army."

"Maybe not," Mason said, "but they can volunteer to help us save lives up on the mountains where General Bragg is in danger of being overrun, and where our boys are dying for lack of medical attention."

"No!" Justin choked. "I've given too much already!"

"Pa, we won't fight. We'll just go to handle the horses." Ruff placed his hand on his father's shoulder. "No fighting," he pledged, looking past his father at the road leading toward Chattanooga and the battlefields. "I swear it."

Justin shook his head, not believing a word of it. His eyes shifted from Mason to Houston and finally settled on Ruff. "You boys are *fighters*! Oh, I expect you'll even try to do as you promised, but you won't be able to once you smell gunpowder and death. You'll fight and get yourselves killed, just like Micha and John."

Mason shook his head vigorously. "Pa, I swear that once the horses are delivered and hitched to those ambulances and supply wagons, I'll send Houston and Ruff back to you. All right?"

After a long moment, Justin finally managed to nod his head. "Come along," he said to no one in particular, "we'll get our Thoroughbreds ready."

But Captain Denton's thin lips twisted in anger. "I want a *dozen* horses! Not one less will do. And I still want that big chestnut stallion in that paddock for my personal mount."

Houston scoffed with derision, "Captain, I've seen some fools in my short lifetime, but none as big as you."

"At least," Denton choked, "my daddy didn't buy my way out of the fighting."

Houston's face twisted with fury and his hand went for the Army Colt strapped to his hip. It was all that Ruff could do to keep his older brother from gunning down the ignorant cavalry officer.

"You *are* a fool," Ruff gritted at the captain when he'd calmed Houston down. "And if you should be lucky enough to survive this war, you'd better pray that you never come across me or any of my family."

Denton wanted to say something. His mouth worked but Ruff's eyes told him he wouldn't live long enough to finish even a single sentence, so the captain just clamped his mouth shut and spun away in a trembling rage.

J.R. ROBERTS
THE
GUNSMITH